Gavin glanced at Brianne, his eyes apprehensive.

A streak of lightning made a jagged dance over the skyscrapers, and a roar of thunder shook the sky. The flowers in the dish gardens bent in the brisk wind. Brianne turned away from the street to give her K-9, Stella, a command so they could move inside. Before she could get to the diner door, the rain started coming down.

Something else started to pour along with the rain. Bullets.

Gavin didn't have time to think. He covered Brianne's body as the dark SUV sped by, one tinted side window in the back open enough to show the tip of a long-barreled revolver. With a silencer.

TRUE BLUE K-9 UNIT:

These police officers fight for justice
with the help of their brave canine partners

With over seventy books published and millions in print, **Lenora Worth** writes award-winning romance and romantic suspense. Three of her books finaled in the ACFW Carol Awards, and her Love Inspired Suspense novel *Body of Evidence* became a *New York Times* bestseller. Her novella in *Mistletoe Kisses* made her a *USA TODAY* bestselling author. Lenora goes on adventures with her retired husband, Don, and enjoys reading, baking and shopping... especially shoe shopping.

Books by Lenora Worth

Love Inspired Suspense

True Blue K-9 Unit

Deep Undercover

Military K-9 Unit

Rescue Operation

Classified K-9 Unit

Tracker
Classified K-9 Unit Christmas
"A Killer Christmas"

Rookie K-9 Unit

Truth and Consequences
Rookie K-9 Unit Christmas
"Holiday High Alert"

Visit the Author Profile page at Harlequin.com for more titles.

DEEP UNDERCOVER

LENORA WORTH

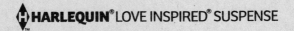
HARLEQUIN® LOVE INSPIRED® SUSPENSE

Special thanks and acknowledgment are given to Lenora Worth
for her contribution to the True Blue K-9 Unit miniseries.

Recycling programs
for this product may
not exist in your area.

LOVE INSPIRED BOOKS

ISBN-13: 978-1-335-23219-9

Deep Undercover

www.Harlequin.com

Printed in U.S.A.

For there is nothing covered, that shall not be revealed;
neither hid, that shall not be known.
–Luke 12:2

To the men and women of the
New York Police Department.
Thank you all for protecting one of my favorite cities.

ONE

K-9 Officer Gavin Sutherland held tight to his partner Tommy's leash and scanned the crowd, his mind on high alert, his whole body tense as he tried to protect the city he loved. People from all over the world stood shoulder to shoulder along the East River, waiting for the annual Fourth of July fireworks display. This New York tradition held a lot of challenges. He searched again in the park and along the riverfront on the Lower East Side of Manhattan.

The upbeat crowd grew more rowdy as the late afternoon sunshine began to slowly descend beyond the Manhattan skyscrapers to the west. Even with the patriotic excitement of the crowd, anything could go wrong. The setting sun hit asphalt and concrete with a laser-like heat while the merging of people seemed to crush in on all sides.

The smell of someone's perfume wafted up and out over the trees to mingle with the scents of cotton candy, street food and that other unique smell of sweaty humans having too much fun.

His partner, a black-and-white springer spaniel, knew the drill. Tommy worked bomb detection. People were always surprised that a springer could be so focused and sharp. Tommy had been trained to find incendiary devices. Period. End of discussion. His quiet, steady work didn't require barking or bringing attention to himself. He knew to sniff the air and the ground. Sniff, sit, repeat. Be rewarded.

But Gavin didn't have to get defensive about his partner. Tommy lived for bomb detection, play toys and rewards.

Lately, Gavin had been the one who needed defending. He'd worked hard all of his life and done things by the book and yet a few choice words during a time of chaos and grief had put a target on his back. As a member of the NYC K-9 Command Unit, based in Queens, he took his job seriously and he'd like to keep it.

Pushing aside the bitterness he'd tried to shed over the last few months, Gavin studied the immediate crowd. A woman with a curly-haired baby laughing at the man by her side. A kid in a Yankees baseball cap tossing a soccer ball in the air, his expression bored. A man wearing a plaid cap carrying a dark backpack. Two young girls in jeans and flag-embossed shirts shoving through the crowd to get the perfect selfie with the backdrop of the city.

Tommy held his head up and sniffed. Too many scents. "It's okay, boy. You're doing great."

Glancing up, Gavin spotted his backup, K-9 Officer Brianne Hayes, a rookie who had been paired with him to continue gaining experience. Her K-9 graduation ceremony should have taken place in the spring but had been postponed due to a tragic event that had rocked the entire K-9 Unit.

Back in April, their chief, Jordan Jameson, had been found dead under strange circumstances. He'd been murdered, but the death had been staged to look like a suicide. His administrative assistant, Sophie Walters, had discovered a suicide note, supposedly from Jordan, the morning of the scheduled graduation. Soon after, his body had been found. But they all knew Jordy had not committed suicide. The whole department was on a mission to find out who'd killed him. But a few key officers were *not* on the case. Jordan had three brothers in the K-9 Unit, and though they were naturally more driven than anyone to find the killer, the Jamesons had been assigned to other cases to avoid conflicts of interest.

No one had forgotten how Gavin had complained about being passed over as chief when the position had been given to Jordan. He and Jordan went way back but they hadn't been close in years. Differences in style going back to their days in training at the Police Academy. Ancient history, but Gavin had learned the hard way not to air his grievances—not with so many Jamesons around to remember every angry word he'd uttered about losing out on the promotion.

They'd both graduated and become police officers. Jordan had gotten married to a good woman who was now pregnant and a widow. Gavin had worked with him, practically side by side, and watched him prosper but had always wondered why Jordan managed to stay one step ahead of him. Now Jordan was dead. Gavin's resentment seemed silly and frivolous. The guilt of that ate at him.

When Jordan became chief, Gavin voiced that resentment. Just another thing between them. Then, shortly after his death, Jordan's position had been given to his brother, Noah Jameson. Gavin had complained again, blurting out his feelings without even thinking. So much for not airing his grievances. After that, Jordan's brothers and the department had unofficially deemed him a person-of-interest in Jordy's death. Unbelievable. He'd been easily cleared—he'd been on duty working a big fund-raising event in Manhattan the night before Jordan had disappeared and his roommate had verified he was home the next morning when Jordan went missing on a jog—but things might not ever be the same.

"Hey, Sutherland, want a bottled water?" Brianne asked.

"Sure, Hayes. Bring it."

Gavin tamped down his resentment about not being promoted, then said a prayer for patience and acceptance. He had to take the high road on this and see things through by helping to find the real killer. He might not have been Jordy's buddy like in the old days, but he sure hadn't killed the man. Now he worked twice as hard as anyone in the department to show his worth. So here he stood on a national holiday, hot, tired and wishing he was out on a boat somewhere.

Brianne headed toward him, her auburn hair caught up in a severe bun. He'd noticed her hair when she'd had it down. Straight and sweeping her shoulders in a soft sheen of deep red. That fire-colored hair matched her fierce determination to prove herself since she was one of only a few female K-9 officers in the city that never slept.

Brianne's partner, Stella, was also in training with the K-9 handlers. The gentle yellow Lab had been pregnant a few months ago when she'd arrived in New York, a gift from the Czech Republic. She'd given birth to eight puppies that had all been farmed out to various officers and their families for socialization and possible future training as either K-9s or service dogs.

Brianne had taken on the job of training Stella in the basics, hoping to someday use her in bomb detection. They'd already started practicing—sniffing explosives, getting a treat and then doing it all over again. Once the dog learned she'd be rewarded for finding that particular scent, they'd move on from sit–stay–pay training to seek–find–reward. Stella now trained at the center and soon she'd be training doing the same thing Tommy specialized in—searching out bombs. Brianne had a way with animals from what he'd heard. Her smile had a way of calming him, Gavin had to admit.

"Thanks," he said now as she handed him the ice-cold water, her lips pursed in professional determination.

"I've been along the perimeters of the park," she said, her golden-brown eyes moving over a thousand faces, her heart-shaped face glowing with a sheen of perspiration. "Nothing out of the ordinary. Hot and humid and crowded. Can't wait for the show."

Gavin smiled at the droll sarcasm and gulped down half the water. Then he poured some in his hand for Tommy to drink. The spaniel lapped it up and wagged his tail. Brianne had already done the same with Stella.

Scanning the area again, he said, "I think the crowd grows every year. Standing-room only tonight."

Brianne wiped a hand across her brow. "Stella keeps fidgeting and sniffing. She needs to get used to this."

"Give her time. She's a rookie like you."

Brianne gave him a mock frown. "And you got stuck with me today."

He didn't mind that but he grinned and played along. "I drew the short straw."

Or at least it felt that way at times, but not today. He'd had a thing for Brianne Hayes since he'd noticed her on her first day of K-9 training. But he'd never acted on his feelings because they worked together and because this job demanded his full attention. They mostly picked on each other and flirted in a playful way. Fine by Gavin. He'd dated off and on but most women couldn't handle his long hours or dark moods.

"*I* drew the short straw," she shot back. "I'd rather be sitting on my tiny back porch with the sprinkler wetting my feet. But Stella and me, we can handle you."

As if she'd heard them talking about her, Stella stopped and lifted her nose into the air, a soft growl emitting from her throat.

Brianne held tight to the leash. "Steady, girl. You'll need to contain that when the fireworks start."

But Stella didn't quit. The big dog tugged forward, her nose sniffing both air and ground.

Gavin watched the Labrador, wondering what kind of scent she'd picked up. Then Tommy alerted, going still except for his wagging tail that acted like a warning flag, his body trembling in place, his nose in the air. A whiff he recognized had hit his odor receptors and sent an alert to his somatosensory cortex so he could process the smell. And it had to be a familiar smell.

"Something's up," Gavin whispered to Brianne. "He's picked up a signature somewhere."

Brianne whispered low. "As in a bomb scent?"

"That's his specialty."

Gavin checked her to make sure she wouldn't panic. Instead of panic, he saw something else in her eyes. Apprehension and anticipation. Brianne's adrenaline faintly shouted at him.

Stella's, too. The rookie knew enough training to expect a reward soon.

"This can't be good," Gavin whispered, watching the crowd. A mass of people side by side. With a bomb nearby, full-out chaos would hit. They'd have to work quietly and quickly to get this situation under control. "We need to verify and contain." He did a sweep of the area. "If we find something, we need to call for backup immediately, okay?"

She nodded and did her own scan of the area.

"We'd better get to work," she said as they both let their partners take the lead, guiding them in a rush through the crowd. "We might not have much time."

It didn't take long to find what the dogs had alerted on. The man Gavin had spotted earlier wearing the plaid cap and carrying a black backpack.

He wasn't carrying the backpack now.

Gavin leaned toward Brianne. "We need to keep an eye on that man up ahead. Don't let him get lost in the crowd. You follow him, and Tommy and I can search for the backpack." Hurrying ahead, he reached for his radio to alert the other NYPD officers in the area.

Brianne nodded, her gaze zooming in on the man pushing through toward the south. "Think he's the one?"

Gavin didn't take his eyes off the man. "Yeah, I do."

The woman he'd noticed earlier sat with her baby girl on a crowded bench, her child in her arms. The kid with the soccer ball kicked it into the air. The ball got lost in the fray, but someone caught it and sent it back to the kid.

"We need to stay calm and see what he does next," he said to Brianne. "See where he goes. The dogs could be wrong, but I doubt that. Stay on the radio."

Tommy alerted again, his eyes on the man ahead but then the dog lifted his nose in the air and changed courses. Gavin pushed his way through shoulder-to-shoulder people, some laughing and ignoring him, some glaring at him full-force. He'd only made it a few feet. Not good.

Gavin stayed focused, trying to keep his eyes on the man who seemed oblivious to all the people shoving at him or to Brianne following him. They got caught up in a large group of teenagers pushing forward around a big oak tree.

Tommy ignored the girls and kept tugging toward the tree. Gavin spotted the backpack, zipped up and sitting on a beach towel by the tree. Tommy headed to it, dug his paws in and lifted his eyes back to Gavin. He didn't need to inspect the bag. If Tommy detected a bomb, Gavin believed him.

"Good work, Tommy."

Gavin called Tommy back away from the area and took in the scene. People all around. He started pushing, trying to guide them away. "Excuse me, folks. Need to clear the area, please."

But he didn't have to say a word. People in New York knew this drill only too well. A man pointed and shouted after he saw Tommy and Gavin—and the backpack. "Suspicious package."

Then someone else started shoving and running away. "Bomb!"

"Go," Gavin called, waving his arms. "Leave the area." Then he stood and spotted Brianne up ahead. She'd already lifted her phone off her waist clip, her eyes meeting his.

"Get back," Gavin shouted, since people were beginning to whisper and stare. "Clear the area," he ordered, lifting his arms to wave to the people near the bench while he and Tommy kept a safe distance away. "Clear the area. Move away from the riverfront."

Brianne and Stella whizzed back toward him. He heard her radio it in through her mic. "10-33 in progress. East River Park. Intersection of East Houston and FDR."

"Stay back, Bree," he called. "Keep searching for the suspect."

She nodded and, giving Gavin one last glance, turned back to her search.

Gavin kept his hand up to keep anyone from approaching too close and he made sure he and Tommy were a safe distance away. The crowd parted and scattered, parents screaming, searching for children, the group of teenaged girls taking off like a pack to get out of the way, families grabbing each other and pushing through the masses.

In the meantime, he radioed for patrol officers to keep the crowd back and listened in on further instructions until the bomb squad arrived. He could expect to see a whole slew of law enforcement agencies arrive soon, including the FBI, ATF and the New York City Fire Department, just in case. Dispatch had already alerted officers up and down the riverfront on both sides of the firework barges. Unless they found more suspicious packages, the show would go on. But it might be delayed if this turned out to be more than a lone, random act.

Gavin prayed that wouldn't be the case.

People were running, screaming, shoving. The little boy with the soccer ball fell and cried out in pain. Someone helped him up while his ball went flying and dropped into the frightened crowd. The woman with the baby abandoned her stroller and took off running, holding her wailing child close to her shoulder. Her husband called after her and caught up to hold his family tight.

People shuffled to get away, some tripping and getting up while others stopped to help. An elderly man pushed a woman in a wheelchair. Too close.

Gavin hurried with Tommy toward the couple, hoping to get them away from the backpack, his heart pumping.

But before he could get to them, a boom and flash, smoke all around, people screaming and shouting, calling out to their loved ones. Gavin felt the blowback hit him in the gut, knocking him down. He stumbled while Tommy leaped into the air and fell over Gavin.

His ears ringing, Gavin sat up and rubbed Tommy's fur. "Thank you, boy. Good boy." His partner appeared intact and ready to get back on the job.

Gavin moved toward the smoke, searching for the old man who'd been pushing the woman in the wheelchair. Had they managed to get out of the way?

Tommy sniffed as they neared the area, the acrid smell from the explosion causing people to cough. The backpack had been incinerated. Gone. A black hole covered the spot where the blanket still burned. Searching for the wheelchair, Gavin also looked for Brianne and Stella. The last time he'd seen them they were coming back toward the tree.

The smoke settled enough that he saw the old man sitting on the ground by the wheelchair, his forehead bleeding. He and the woman held hands. Both safe and sound and looking at each other.

Gavin headed toward them to make sure they were okay. "You folks all right?"

The man nodded, still holding his wife's hand. "Forty-eight years together. We're tougher than we look, son."

Gavin talked to them in a calm voice, making sure they were both okay and telling them help was on the way. Their love for each other was evident—like a punch to the gut but in a good way.

Then he glanced up and saw Brianne and Stella coming from the other direction, Brianne limping. But she gave him a thumps-up.

"Lost the suspect when someone in the crowd accidentally knocked me to the ground. Heading back," she reported over the radio. Brianne turned toward Gavin, Stella dancing at her feet. Shrugging, she held up her hands in defeat.

They'd lost the bomber. But the entire NYPD now had his description from Gavin. The man could easily detonate another bomb at any minute, though. But Gavin had to wonder if he'd planned the attack to hit when the fireworks started going off. Worst-case scenario. Yet the bomb hadn't done a lot of damage. Someone out for kicks? Or sending a warning to the city?

He let out a breath of relief but knew it would be short-lived. He had to go over this bomb scene and do a search for the man they'd spotted. What if he'd planted more bombs?

"Are you okay?" he asked through the radio.

Brianne hurried toward where he stood and nodded to him, her expression intense as she allowed Stella to do her job.

He hadn't realized until that moment that he really wanted Brianne to be okay.

Glancing back at the old couple, he wondered what it would be like to hold someone's hand at that age and still be in love.

Knowing he needed to search for more bombs, he hurried to meet Brianne, his mind still on that strong, courageous couple.

TWO

Off in the distance and after a long delay, the fireworks finally started. The areas on both sides of the river were now being heavily patrolled by the NYPD and several other law enforcement personnel from various agencies. But thankfully no other devices had been found along the river or in any of the parks, and most of the people on both sides were never aware that they'd searched for bombs. The fireworks barge had been cleared. The show would go on, but the search for the suspect would intensify. Reporters hovered near the cordoned-off areas, wanting the scoop. A few brave people stood behind the police lines, determined to see the fireworks now that the area had technically been cleared. But most of the people who'd been crammed into this area had either gone home or moved to another safer location.

Not a good situation, Brianne thought as they walked the perimeters that had been marked with police tape. The bomb fragments were being gathered, piece by piece, by the bomb squad and so far no other explosive devices had been found. The lab would go over every shred to find clues or markers. No word on the suspect they'd seen earlier. .

Random? Or deliberate? She hoped they'd find the suspect somewhere in the city.

Brianne still shuddered each time she thought about the device that had exploded less than two hours ago in the haze of the coming dusk. If Stella and Tommy hadn't alerted...

But that was the job. Taking care of this city. New trainee Stella had done her part and she'd been rewarded with her treat, which involved a ball and a few minutes of playtime, followed by a doggie treat. They'd have more playtime when they got home. Aggravated that she'd let the suspect get by her, Brianne looked up and found Gavin and Tommy heading toward her. Glad that they were still alive, she tried not to think about how Gavin made her feel.

"What a night," he said, fatigue darkening his eyes.

"And it's not over," she replied. "We don't leave until everyone else does."

"Could be a while."

Brianne had not been happy to be partnered with this man. He had a reputation around headquarters for being an overly ambitious hothead. But she had to admit that today he'd been professional and courageous. And caring. He'd personally made sure the elderly couple that had been nearest to the explosion had both been checked over by the paramedics and cleared. Then he'd seen to it that they had an escort home, not a taxi but a cruiser.

Now Brianne wondered if a big teddy bear hid behind that gruff, fierce exterior. Gavin was good-looking in a don't-mess-with-me way, his hair a rich tousled brown, his eyes almost black, his attitude tough and untouchable. Maybe she'd misjudged her coworker, but then her last boyfriend had explained to her that she needed to work on her trust issues.

Even though she'd caught him cheating with her now-ex-best friend. Yeah, she had a few trust issues. But more than that, her determination and ambition matched that of the man walking with her right now. And that meant no love life. Too messy.

"You might need some downtime later tonight," he said. "It's always rough when things get this heavy."

Whirling to face him, Brianne scoffed. "You don't think I have the mettle to handle this, Gavin?"

"I didn't say that," he replied, clearly confused. "We had an intense situation, but you handled it like a pro."

Anger gaining strength, she glared up at him. "I am a pro. I haven't gotten my official graduation certificate yet, but that doesn't mean I can't do the job."

"I said all of that wrong," he replied, looking adorably sheepish. "You're tough, Bree. We can all see that. You work harder than any of us in training and on the streets."

"You mean, for a woman, right?"

"I hadn't noticed," he retorted, with a trace of a smile.

"Are you laughing at me, Sutherland?"

"No, ma'am."

"Now you're calling me *ma'am*?"

"Look, I'm headed for coffee and something to eat once we're off duty. I'm bushed and I'm starving and my adrenaline has about run its course. You're welcome to come with." Checking his watch, he added, "Our shift should have ended an hour ago."

Feeling contrite and a bit embarrassed, Brianne again wondered about Gavin Sutherland. She hesitated for her own reasons, but he took it the wrong way.

"Okay, I get it," he said, walking ahead of her. "You obviously don't want to hang around with a piranha like me."

"You don't look that dangerous," she said, catching up with him. "I don't think of you in that way."

No, right now she thought of him in a whole new way. Something that had more teeth than any old scary fish. Mentally doing a shakedown, she pushed all of that away for now. Her adrenaline had drained away, too.

"Then what do you think of me?"

His question caught her off guard. She'd noticed him. It would be hard for any woman to skip right over a man like him. But she knew better than to get involved with a coworker, especially since he was right. She'd worked hard in training and on the job to show everyone she meant business. She'd taken on the task of training Stella to make some points, but now she loved the dog with all of her heart and she planned to make Stella the best bomb-detection dog in this city. Stella had done a good job today, so Brianne knew her gut instincts had been spot on.

"Can't even say it?"

Holding tight to Stella, Brianne shot him another glare and got her mind back on the conversation. "Yes, I can say it. I don't know you that well, but I think you were given a bum rap. You might want to get promoted, but you wouldn't kill anyone to make that happen. You're too loyal to the department for that and besides, you have a solid alibi for when Jordan disappeared."

Giving her an uncertain frown that made his eyebrows shift up, he said, "Thank you, I think."

He took off and followed Tommy, his whole body on alert. Maybe the man just needed a friend.

"Look," she said, tired but still full of enough tension to know that this man made her pulse beat a little faster. "it's been a long hot day and I'm going home when I'm done. Then we get right back to it tomorrow."

He didn't argue with her. "Yep. I need to find some food and then I'm going to go over my report one more time. We have to keep looking for the man in the plaid hat."

"Because he could strike again," she replied, her eyes holding his.

Gavin nodded. "Yes, I have a bad feeling this might only be the beginning."

The next morning, Griffin's Diner was hopping as usual. People still enjoying what was left of the Fourth of

July weekend were lined up at the double French doors of the quaint brick building located on a bustling corner near 94th Street in Queens.

Brianne had walked the couple blocks over from the K-9 Command Unit in search of some good coffee and a nice shady spot on the patio.

The old red bricks of the restaurant had mellowed to a deep burgundy over the years. Brianne remembered coming here with her parents as a child and seeing the pictures on the wall of fallen officers, one of them a brother to the owner, Louis Griffin. Most of the K-9s in service now had been named after those who'd died while on duty, including Gavin's partner, Tommy, named after Officer Tommy McNeill.

The diner had been in the Griffin family for generations and easygoing baseball fanatic Louis "Lou" Griffin was a fixture in the place, along with his blunt-talking wife, Barbara, who had a no-nonsense attitude and took care of everything from bookkeeping to settling down unruly customers. Their daughter, Violet, a friend of Brianne's, worked with them when she wasn't at her regular job as a ticket agent at the airport. They'd lost their five-year-old son to meningitis nearly twenty years ago. She often wondered if that's why they all poured so much love into this old building.

Brianne moved around to the right corner where an alfresco area lined with potted dish gardens led to the private space designated for the NYPD and the K-9 team's four-legged partners. She opened one of the matching French doors there, smiling at the etched plaque over the door— *The Dog House, Reserved for New York's Finest.*

She headed inside to see if Violet was working and get that big cup of coffee but stopped when she heard her name.

"Hey, Bree."

Turning, she saw Gavin approaching, Tommy moving ahead.

Holding the door, she tried to hide her surprise. "What are you doing here?"

He pointed to where a big red umbrella cast a shade over one of the square metal tables near a side street. "I never ate last night. I'm going to order a big breakfast." Then he lifted his chin. "Grab your coffee and meet me back out here. It's cloudy and not too hot yet. Lou's got the rotating fan going already."

"Outside it is, then," she replied, again noticing her good-looking coworker while she wondered why she'd stopped here today, of all mornings. Unless someone else showed up, they had the whole patio to themselves. Not that she minded. More like *too intimate*. Brianne wanted to keep things light and professional. But…a chance meeting over coffee, coworkers did that, right?

When she came back with a to-go cup, Gavin didn't dare hold out her chair, even though he looked as if he might. They both sat down at the same time, facing toward the street, their partners curling up at their feet to wait for water and a special treat from Lou.

"So how ya doing?" he asked, his attitude more relaxed and laid back today.

"Peachy," she replied. "Slept like a rock."

"I never know if you're being sarcastic or serious," he replied, smiling over at her.

"And I'll never tell you which."

She hadn't slept much at all. She kept reliving the moment when that bomb had exploded. But she'd made notes each time she remembered something and she aimed to get back to work. Like right now.

Barbara came out with a coffee pot. "Anyone hungry?"

She refilled Gavin's mug, her question causing Brianne's stomach to growl loudly. "What else can I bring you guys?"

"Pancakes," they both said, laughing.

"Pancakes it is," she said, taking her pen out from behind her ear, loose strands of curling brown hair with gray edging escaping her bun. "How 'bout some bacon with that?"

"None for me," Brianne said. "I hadn't planned on staying."

"Double stack," Gavin replied to Barbara.

Brianne shook her head and smiled up at Barb. "Hey, is Violet here this morning?"

"Not yet," Barb said with a smile. "But she's due to stop by any minute now. We're going to talk wedding plans. Have you seen her ring?"

"I have," Brianne replied. "She and Zach seem so happy."

"They are—finally," Barb said. "Took them all of their lives living next to each other and then almost getting killed by some drug dealer to figure it out."

When Barbara walked away, Gavin looked over at Brianne. "Zach needed someone in his life right now. It's been tough on all of the Jameson brothers, losing Jordan."

"I agree," Brianne said, remembering Jordan's funeral and how his brothers had stood so solemn and strong. "Now if we could just find his killer."

"Yeah, I want that, too." Gavin looked down, probably remembering being heavily questioned about Jordan's death since the whole unit knew he'd been bitter about not being promoted to chief. But she didn't broach that subject. He'd been cleared, and that was good enough for her.

He didn't offer up any explanations. Instead, he switched gears. "So you like pancakes, but you don't eat meat?"

"I do but…bacon is addictive. I try to pace myself."

"And why are you in such a hurry to get away from me?"

"I'm not," she said, thinking she needed to do just that. "I came by to get some coffee and chat with my friend. But I remembered some things about last night so I jotted notes to add to my official report. I wasn't planning on hanging around for a big breakfast. I want to do a search and see if I can get a match on that bomber."

He took a sip of his coffee and did the cop scan that came naturally. Trucks whizzed by, vehicles honked, people hurried down the sidewalks. A typical day in the city. "I figured you'd head right to headquarters this morning."

"I went over my report early this morning," she said, nodding. "And I have lots of questions, but I needed some of Barbara's strong coffee first."

"What kind of questions?" he asked. "I have a few of my own but we'll need to see what the lab's found, too."

"That guy in the plaid hat. Gavin, he walked right past us."

"Yeah, I know. Taunting the police? Daring us to see him?"

She took a long drink of coffee. "I did some research online. No other recent reports of bomb threats or bomb scares, but there does seem to be a rash of small explosions all over the city lately."

Gavin tensed up and turned wary. "Such as?"

"In buildings, parking garages, things like that. They've all been explained away as accidents. A boiler explosion here, a garage fire there, several construction fires. But no bomb threats or actual bombs—except possibly at one particular site." She paused. "A site that you and Tommy worked, Gavin. Williamsburg. A boiler exploded in the basement. Why were you called in?"

He didn't flinch, and he didn't look away. "I heard the call on the radio. I happened to be nearby so I went."

"What did you find?"

He looked away this time. She'd read the report. Possible incendiary device. Unsubstantiated. Not enough evidence.

"Gavin, what do you know about that explosion?"

Giving her a confused stare, he asked, "What are you getting at?"

"Nothing. Because I have nothing. But I'm concerned we might start seeing more bombings in the parks or in other big crowded events. Maybe even in buildings. I don't want that to happen but if it does, we'll need to be prepared for a serial bomber."

His expression changed, turning serious and standoffish.

"You think I'm crazy?" she asked, her fingers drumming the table and causing both Stella and Tommy to glance up. That or she'd stepped on his sensitive toes by taking some initiative?

"No. But, Bree, we have bomb threats all the time. It's part of living in New York and most of them are never reported to the public. We handle things to keep everyone safe. This could have been a prank by someone bored and looking for blood or…we could have a terrorist toying with us. We need to be prepared, yes, but we also have to be careful."

"I'm going to be careful," she said. "But I'm also going to find out what I can about this bomber."

When he looked away again, she beamed in on him like a laser pen. "You know something already, don't you, Gavin?"

He shook his head. "I'm not good with words or explaining things. You've seen me blurt out my feelings right in front of everyone."

"Yeah, I have. But now you're clammed-up and this has to be about last night. You need to fill me in. So start talking."

Gavin took a sip of black coffee, completely unaware of her inner turmoil. But he did seem to have some of his own. "You were a pro yesterday."

Oh, so now he tried to put a spin on this and build up her confidence? "I let the suspect get away."

"No, you didn't. He slipped away with a crowd of people, oldest trick in the book."

"I want to find him."

"I do, too," Gavin said. "And believe it or not, I agree with you. We could wind up having a serial bomber on our hands. And yes, he could be the man who walked right past us yesterday."

"But you weren't going to tell me that because…?"

He looked directly at her now. "I have to sort things out in my mind and make sure I'm right before I jump to conclusions."

"You don't trust me."

"It's not like that."

She shouldn't have been disappointed. This job could be competitive at times and she had to stay one step ahead. She'd given herself a good pep talk on the way over here, so she squelched any mixed messages she might have scrambled in her brain and gave him her I'm-all-in smile. "Then what is it like, Gavin?"

She drank her coffee while she waited, too many questions popping in her head while sweat popped out along her spine.

"I don't know yet. But if you listen to me and let me

explain, we might be able to crack this case together," he said, his tone pure business, his gaze steady on her face.

So he did have a plan and he did know more than he'd let on. "How can I help?"

"By pretending to be my wife," he said.

And he was dead serious.

THREE

Brianne swallowed so fast the coffee went down the wrong way and she started coughing.

Gavin watched her, his expression puzzled and confused and kind of comical. She took a sip of water and tried to clear her throat before Lou came rushing out to give her the Heimlich maneuver.

"Would you mind repeating that?" she asked, wiping her eyes.

"Are you okay?"

Nodding, she lifted her right hand to wave him on because she really wanted to hear this. A couple of uniforms came through, nodded and headed inside.

The sky had darkened, and she thought she'd seen a streak of lightning to the west. Traffic noises merged with thunder.

"It's for a case," he said, handing her another paper napkin to wipe her eyes. "I mean, it might be this case."

"Involving the bomber from last night?"

"I don't know yet. We'll have to figure that out together."

"Why me?" she asked, still confused.

"I'm not an undercover cop," he said. "Not even a detective. I can't give up my identity to go undercover but I can snoop around. I just need a cover for a few weeks."

Barbara came out with their meal and refilled their coffee, pretending she hadn't noticed all the coughing drama. But she shot Brianne a knowing smile. "Looks like rain," she said, glancing at the billowing gray clouds. "Better eat up."

Stella and Tommy sniffed the air. *Bacon?*

She felt their pain. Brianne watched Barbara go back inside and then grabbed a slice of crisp bacon. "I think I'm gonna need this."

"I've been following a lead," he explained between bites of fluffy pancakes and the best bacon in New York.

Or at least it tasted that way to Brianne each time she swiped a strip. Stress eating was her thing, after all. She'd have to run the bacon off later. And she'd have to run off the strange currents circulating through her system, too. Why, oh why had she been paired with this man?

Work. Focus on work. "What kind of lead?"

"A few months ago, we established that a person noted as a master bomb-maker might be back in New York and that he could possibly be the one who set off the boiler explosion that caused part of the apartment building you mentioned to wind up in pieces. One person killed and three hospitalized. Tommy and I were the first to arrive on the scene because I had dinner with a friend at a nearby restaurant. Tommy alerted and we found fragments of what looked like the makings of a bomb. Pieced things together but the FBI and Homeland Security took over the case."

"The explosion in Williamsburg?" she asked, gaining interest. "An older apartment building. They couldn't figure out what had caused the boiler to explode but this report says possible tampering. They never found a suspect."

"*We* never found a suspect. Tommy and I gave it our best shot and we found evidence of an incendiary device but no trace of the person who might have done it." He shrugged and shook his head. "I had to let it go."

"Maybe the department will get a lead soon."

"They won't, and for several reasons," he said. "First,

we only have a written report from the other agencies and I had to ask special permission for that. Plus, this possible bomber is like a ghost, but my confidential informant—we call him Beanpole because he's so skinny—told me he's heard things about that explosion being deliberate. Someone wanted that building destroyed. He thinks he's seen the man who did it and he described him to me. If it's who I think it is, he's known as the Tick—a double meaning. His bombs don't always tick but he grips his target and won't let go until the job is done. I'm talking taunting, stalking, harassing and then…boom."

"Like a tick on skin?"

"Yes. Hard to find and even harder to shake."

She almost shuddered but lifted her shoulder instead. "Not a good image."

"No. This man is dangerous. He's not considered a terrorist and he's not connected to any sleeper cells as far as we can tell. But someone could be hiring him to sabotage or damage buildings so they can be condemned. That forces people out so they can buy the property at rock-bottom prices and rebuild on it, making a fortune. That makes him a domestic terrorist in my book, him and whoever is paying him to do this."

He stopped, waiting for her to bolt. But Brianne sat with her eyes on him, giving him her complete attention.

"After that explosion, I did some research and found a pattern that seems to match his MO. I found one report from a building in Chicago—a gas explosion. Blasted but no foul play found. Six months later, the property had switched hands and a fancy new condominium building went up. And another in Atlanta, same pattern. A fire in the basement that got out of hand, ruled as an electrical fire. A few months later, the place had been razed to build a new high-rise condo building."

"So you see a pattern developing?"

"Yes. Those incidents have all the markings of the Tick. He disguises his bombs to make them look like something else—a gas leak, a boiler blowing up, an accidental construction fire. Once that's over and done, the buildings change hands pretty quickly. The previous owners might get an insurance settlement but an offer to buy them out would sure add to that. And I think they're being persuaded in other ways, too."

"Intimidation?" She shook her head. "Violet's mentioned Lou being harassed lately. Something about gentrification."

"Yes, that kind of thing. The threat of another explosion, rumors that scare tenants away."

"So…you've been researching this because…?"

He took a swig of coffee and checked the clouds coming in. "I didn't like leaving the case unsolved, and I need something to prove I'm not just out to get promoted. I really care about this case. I'm ambitious, true. But…this is dangerous stuff. The Williamsburg explosion turned out to be more powerful—enough to take down a small building and kill a woman. Tommy alerted and our partners are rarely wrong on these things. But…we didn't find enough proof."

"So how is he getting away with this?"

"I think someone higher up is hiring him to scare property owners. He's meticulous in hiding his tracks but now he's getting bolder. Bombers like notoriety, but they don't want to get caught so they prefer to leave little signatures but not much evidence."

"So these real estate agents are trying to scare vulnerable people out of their apartments and homes so they can raze them and build?"

"Yes. They want the property, but not the buildings."

He sat silently, as if weighing his next words. "They make people back off on contracts or force owners to sell quietly and quickly. They've got a system of intimidation and bullying tactics and the bomber is just the tip of the iceberg. No one can prove anything so the owners cave and wash their hands of the entire mess."

"So it's not just about the bomber? You want these corrupt real estate agents to end their bullying ways."

"I do, for so many reasons." Looking out over the street, he let out a sigh. "The woman who died in that explosion worked with my grandmother at a nearby hospital. I knew her, Bree. Helen Proctor. She lived in Williamsburg all of her life and most of that time in the apartment she shared with her husband before he died. She was good to me when my grandmother got sick and…after she passed away." Twisting his napkin, he added, "I knew she lived there but…but I couldn't believe it when they brought her out in a body bag."

And right after that, Jordan Jameson had died and Gavin had been put through the wringer as a possible suspect. No wonder he seemed to have a big chip on his shoulder.

More like the weight of the world.

"I'm sorry, Gavin. So sorry." Brianne's heart burned with understanding. She'd heard Gavin's grandmother had raised him after his mother left him as an infant. She didn't bring up any of that, though. "So this is personal for you?"

"Very," he admitted. "At the time, Jordan knew about my connection to Helen, so I asked if I could investigate the alleged bombing on the side, on my own time if needed."

"And he agreed to that?"

"He did after I explained—Helen Proctor didn't deserve

to die that way. He knew, Noah knows and now you. I'd like to keep it that way. No one else, okay?"

"Okay." She could see how much this meant to him. But how far would he be willing to go?

"So the chief went along with your plan?"

"He told me to be careful. Jordan and I go way back, but we had a falling out when we were in the academy together and later, as everyone knows, I resented him getting promoted. I think he initially gave the go-ahead to this because we both felt bad about what happened—a stupid fight over a training episode. Just too stubborn to apologize."

Brianne could now see why Gavin seemed so solemn at times. She wanted to hear more about what had happened between them, but she'd save that for another time. "You feel guilty about that?"

"Of course I do." Shrugging, he said, "Then I got put on the suspect list regarding his murder. That stung, you know. I wish I'd kept my opinions to myself, but I understand how my complaining looked bad."

"We all know you wouldn't kill Jordan, Gavin. And we have proof that you didn't. I read the report. You worked a swanky fund-raiser in Midtown and both the commissioner and the mayor saw you there. Then you arrived home around midnight and your roommate said you guys talked for an hour and both went to bed. Your vehicle never left your yard until after nine that morning, according to the traffic cameras in the area."

"You read the report?"

"Of course I did. Jordan was last seen at six a.m. But I didn't have to read a report to know the truth."

He shot her a look that held appreciation and admiration. And something else she couldn't read. "Thank you, Bree."

She nodded and took a long sip of coffee.

"So now you're on this quest for two reasons—you knew a woman who died at the hands of this possible bomber and...you owe it to Jordan and now the new chief, his brother Noah, to show your true merit?"

He studied her, probably looking for a judgmental frown. When she didn't give him one, he nodded. "Yes, I guess that's it in a nutshell. This is important to me."

Brianne leaned forward. "So you're after the Tick. What's the plan?"

"Well, I'm after him, but I'm also after the people who've hired him. This is a classic case of intimidation. Mafia-style." Glancing around, he made sure they were alone. "After comparing a couple of random explosions around Manhattan, I've been discreetly asking questions, talking to wealthy investors, stuff like that. We're talking seven figures or more—a lot of money. If someone is sabotaging developers and property owners by bombing buildings so they can step in and take over, it could only get worse from here."

Confused and needing to know the bottom line, she asked, "But Gavin, you're a K-9 cop. You're usually not involved in the investigative part. I can't believe the department agreed to this."

His expression went from hopeful to disappointed in a flash. "I'd been doing this on the side, on my own time, after I got a tip from Beanpole. But I kept Jordy up-to-date." Sighing, he added, "After Jordy went missing and was found dead, I went to Noah to get permission to continue working on this case. You know the rest. This had to be put on hold. We all want to find Jordy's killer. That's top priority for the precinct."

"But you're still working on this, too, clearly."

He nodded and then stared out into the street. "I'm not

hiding it from Noah or anyone else. In fact, I think they're all glad I've got something else to occupy me. Even though I've been cleared of any suspicion in Jordy's death, I can't shake the doubters who still aren't sure."

Beginning to understand, she said, "But if you solve this case, you'd look better in everyone's eyes, right?"

"I hope so. Bree, I didn't always get along with Jordy but…I respected him. He was a good cop and a good leader. I need this—not only because of that, but because this man is getting bolder with each bomb. He has to be stopped."

Brianne didn't know what to say. Good officers knew working without backup was never the best plan. Glad he'd been upfront with the chief, she said, "You shouldn't go it alone. Have you talked to the FBI and Homeland Security any more?"

"They've been informed. Those in charge know Tommy and I are good at what we do. As long as I don't interfere in their cases, I'm clear. I have to report back, of course. Besides, I'm not technically undercover. I've just trying to build a solid case—on my own time and in my own way."

"This is an unusual situation," she said. "I know a lot of detectives who are deep undercover. They give up everything to do their jobs."

"Yes, but my job is bomb detection and…I can't let this one go. Tommy found something at that site, and I think he recognized that man yesterday after Stella alerted. I took this on because my gut tells me this man is so close. And based on Beanpole's vague description of him, I think that could have been him. I haven't figured out why he'd bomb the park, but it could have been a distraction. I can't talk to anyone much about it per Noah's orders, but the NYPD is well aware of the situation and they've got people on it, too. I thought I could trust you, though, since you were there."

"And then you got this wild idea that we could both work this case, possibly undercover as husband and wife?"

"Something like that. It's stupid, I know. But…I need evidence, and most of the detectives I know are swamped and all in on their own cases." He took a sip of coffee. "As you know, I rent out a room in the house in Valley Stream I inherited from my Granny Irene. My roommate's so deep undercover, I get rent money from a PO box and I haven't seen him since he vouched for me three months ago—right before he started this new case."

A streak of lightning made a jagged dance over the skyscrapers and then a roar of thunder shook the sky. The flowers in the dish gardens bent in the brisk wind.

"We'd better get inside," he said, his tone gruff now.

Brianne stood. "I want to hear more," she said. "All of it. Then I'll decide."

"Forget I mentioned it."

She slanted her eyebrow up. "Oh, no. This conversation is not over."

The lightning flashed again. Brianne turned away from the street to give Stella a command so they could move inside.

Before she could get to the door, the rain started coming down. Gavin glanced at an approaching SUV and then back at her, his eyes filling with apprehension.

In the next instance, he jumped across the table and covered her, pushing her down, rain pouring around them.

But something else also poured out along with the rain.

Bullets.

FOUR

Gavin didn't have time to think.

He dove over Brianne, his body covering hers as the dark SUV sped by, one tinted side-window in the back open enough to show the tip of a long-barreled revolver. With a silencer.

But even with that silencer, he could still hear the hiss of a projectile coming straight toward them.

While he held her, bullets ricocheted off bricks and iron, one hitting the umbrella where they'd just been sitting, the force ripping the sturdy canvas apart. After what seemed like a lifetime of seconds, the SUV peeled away, wet tires spinning.

For one moment, everything went silent and then everyone moved at once.

The two officers who'd gone inside just minutes earlier came rushing out, weapons drawn.

"Hey, are you guys okay?"

"Shots fired." Gavin looked down at Brianne. He'd knocked her down so quickly, her hair had tumbled out around her face. "You hit?"

"No, no," she said, her breath rising. "How about you?"

"I'm fine."

"The dogs?"

Gavin checked Stella who sat loyally beside where Brianne had landed, her ears up and her eyes on alert. Tommy did the same. These two weren't trained to attack but they wouldn't back off either if push came to shove. "They're good. A tough combo."

Brianne reached out a hand and touched Stella's furry head. "Good girl."

He sat back and then leaped up, offering her a hand. "Are you sure you're all right?"

"I'm fine," she said, grabbing hold, her hand sending little currents of warmth straight to his heart. "My knee is still bruised and cut from falling yesterday in the park and I'll probably have a bruise on my elbow where I hit the concrete when...when you dived over me."

"Sorry," he said, unable to stop staring at her. "I saw the barrel of a gun and went into action."

"We'd better stay in action," she said, her expression hard to read. "We should contain the scene."

Gavin looked around, his mind refocusing. Lou came hurrying out, oblivious to the rain or any shooters, his salt-and-pepper hair standing straight up. "Get inside," he said, worry in his tone.

One of the patrol officers nodded. "Go on. We've called it in, but we didn't see the vehicle or the shooter."

"The vehicle—a black Denali," Gavin replied. "I didn't get the tag numbers. I'll see if I can remember any details when we file a report. Could have been random."

"Right," the younger of the two said. "Two cops sitting on a patio. An easy target."

Lou studied the street, his expression grim. "Who knows these days? We had that shooting when Sophie Walters was targeted, but that man's dead now. Then Eva Kendall's nephew Mikey got taken from here, remember? Glad they found the boy safe and sound."

He shrugged and then held his hands up in defeat. "Maybe I should just sell the place." He turned to go back inside but whirled around. "This time might have been a warning for me. Someone really wants to buy this property, but I keep refusing to sell. Different real estate agents come by all the time, smart-mouthing."

Gavin shot a glance to Brianne. "Lou, are you being strong-armed?"

Lou shook his head. "I have been but I handled it. Just braggish folks with business cards and big offers. You know, gentrification. As if anyone around here wants to become more refined, know what I mean? I refused all offers, of course. But today, they might have fired their first warning shot directly at me. If this keeps up, we'll lose business and I'll be forced to shut things down."

"Like I said," Gavin replied to the officers. "Random? Or maybe not."

"We've got this," the other one said. "Get inside and dry off."

"Bree, let's go in and talk about what happened."

She fixed her hair, her skin and uniform soaked. "What's to talk about? They shot at *us*, right? Whether they were targeting Lou or us, we're in this. I'm not going inside."

He nodded, worrying, calculating.

Brianne studied the porch and the street. "I don't think this was random, Gavin. So I'd like to help process the scene."

"We can agree on that," he said, his tone grim. "Did you see anything?"

"No. I should have been more alert."

"Except I had you distracted with my lamebrain plan."

"We're not done with that," she reminded him.

The rain softened into a drizzle but since they were both drenched they didn't care. "Let's check for bullet fragments," she said. "The rain might not let up and it's washing away evidence."

"I saw a black SUV, a late model Denali. I didn't get a license plate number. But then we see those all over town all the time. Hired drivers."

"And Lou doesn't have video footage to the street."

"Nope. But the transportation department does. I'll get Danielle's team on that."

They walked the patio, lifting bullet fragments for balistics and taking statements. The rain ended and a hot scalding sun came out to make their wet uniforms even stickier. The patrol officers cordoned off the patio until they'd cleared the scene.

Lou brought out water and offered them coffee. "Find anything?"

"Nope," Gavin said. "But we'll try to figure it out." Then he touched Lou's beefy arm. "I'll need to sit down with you later and hear more about the people trying to buy you out."

Lou shrugged. "People have been trying to buy me out since I opened the diner over thirty years ago. I don't plan on going anywhere. Not without a fight, at least."

Gavin wondered about that. And he wondered if the people who seemed to be targeting Lou might also be after Gavin now, too. Did they know he'd been asking around? Did they assume he was snooping on Lou's behalf?

"Can I get you anything else?" the older man asked, clearly rattled. Barbara came out and tried to tug them all inside, her face etched in worry.

They worked the scene in quiet and then went inside to interview the patrons and Lou and Barb. No one had anything new to add. Most of the diners had been cleared to leave.

"We've had a couple of real estate agents handing out cards and telling us how much we can get for the property," Barb said. "We didn't think anything of it and Lou politely told them we didn't want to sell."

"They weren't polite," Lou told them. "But you know how that goes. Firm and with greed glowing in their eyes. I threw their cards in the trash."

He barely remembered what they looked like, so not much to go on there. "Violet was here the other day when a woman came by and handed me a card. She might be able to describe the woman better. I had people shouting for food so I hurried away."

As if on cue, Violet showed up, pushing her way through the bystanders and the yellow police tape. Hugging her parents close, she turned to Gavin. "What happened?"

Gavin brought her up to speed. "Everyone is okay but I need to ask you some questions."

"Sure," she said, her dark hair caught up in a clip. "What's up?"

"Look, no one was hurt but Lou says they've been approached by some pesky real estate brokers trying to get them to sell out. Lou thinks the bullets might have been a warning for you guys. Do you know anything about that?"

"I talked to a woman once," Violet said, her voice shaky, her arm on her father's shoulder. "She was persistent and maybe a little threatening. Do you think they'd resort to this kind of harassment? Are my parents in danger?"

Barb and Lou patted her on the arm. "Honey, we're fine," Lou said over and over.

Gavin needed to consider that angle, but he didn't have the answer right now. "I think it could have been for Bree and me, but we can't be sure." He thanked her for the information.

Assuring her that her parents were okay, he promised

to alert Violet's fiancé, Zach—a fellow K-9 officer—just in case. "We'll keep watch, either way."

"Thanks," Gavin said to Barbara after she'd handed them both a to-go box of fresh food since they hadn't finished their breakfasts. "I'm going back to headquarters."

"Same here," Brianne said. "I drove but I have a clean uniform in my locker."

"I came here first, too, and found a parking place around the corner."

Her brow scrunched. "I'll see you back at the station"

"Okay. Watch your back."

Before they left to go their separate ways, she turned to Gavin. "I don't know why I'm saying this but…I really do want to hear more about your case, Gavin."

"I thought you were against it."

"No, I just like to do things by the book. If you need my help, that's fine. But…we clear it with Noah, understand? Let him know you need me on the case and explain why."

"I don't know—"

"You're already on their radar. If you've been cleared to work on this, that's cool. I need to get clearance, too. We can't be too careful, considering."

"What do you want me to do, Brianne? I took this case and then Jordy died and…I made a mess of things. I need something to focus on."

"We do have something to focus on—finding Chief Jameson's killer and searching for the Fourth of July bomber."

"I want to find the Tick, too. I've just got a hunch that they could be one and the same. And now this. It could all be tied together, especially if they've decided to target Lou, too."

"I want to find that bomber we saw in the park. I don't like this place being shot up, and Lou could be a target now. But we continue to do it by the book or...I'll never work with you again."

She turned and marched off, her shoulders straight, her hair still trying to escape the messy bun she'd managed to fix.

Gavin watched her head to her SUV across the way. He checked the windows of buildings around the area. Had he made a big mistake by telling her what he'd been up to? Now he had to consider someone had just shot at this building. Who? Why?

Lou had been upfront about someone wanting to buy him out, but what if he had been pressured way more than any of them knew?

Hurrying to his vehicle, Gavin got caught up in a traffic jam caused by construction. While he sat there waiting for the workers to finish their task, Gavin thought about his grandmother, Irene. She'd died five years ago, leaving him her home and a modest savings account. His grandmother had raised him after his mother, Phyllis, had given birth out of wedlock. Phyllis, still a teenager, had run away when he'd been only a month old and hadn't come back. Irene, who'd become a widow at an early age, had cared for him and sent him to college, all the while working as a nurse her entire life. She'd only been retired a year or so when her health turned bad.

He'd never had to prove himself to Granny Irene. She loved him with a tough love but he knew he could always count on her. His grandmother lived by faith and she'd planted that seed in his heart. He didn't talk about his faith much, but he tried hard to live up to Irene's strong belief system.

Checking on Tommy in the back, Gavin said, "Hey, boy. We should have walked back to work, huh?"

Tommy woofed his agreement and did a circle inside the kennel. Always ready to roll.

At least he had a solid house with a small yard for Tommy. Small but intact, the two-story wooden row house had a narrow front porch. It belonged to him, no matter how many real estate agents told him he could make a fortune flipping it and selling it.

Maybe that also had something to do with how this particular case bothered him. His grandfather had been a fairly successful businessman and had bought the house, built in the 1940s, for a modest price over fifty years ago.

After his grandfather's death in a traffic accident, his grandmother had raised his wayward mother there. He'd never sell, even if Valley Stream was now a coveted area. But the place stayed in a continuous state of remodeling and updating. It had a nice backyard for Tommy and room enough for the both of them and his rarely-there roommate. That's all Gavin needed.

Or so he'd thought until Brianne had come into his life. Working with her now and then over the last few weeks, helping her to train Stella and getting to know her better had only made him more aware of her. The woman had a sweet heart behind a solid wall of feminine steel.

Holding her there after the shooting this morning, he'd felt something powerful and true, the kind of emotions a man hides inside his heart. Gavin didn't know how to deal with all the possibilities swirling inside his head. He needed to keep a professional attitude regarding Brianne Hayes.

Now he'd put her in a bad position.

He had to trust her. He needed a partner to help him crack this case. A female who could pose as his rich wife so they could attend open houses and get information on properties without looking suspicious. Brianne had the

backbone and the nerves to pull off a high-risk undercover job, but he wondered now if he should put her in
the line of fire.

Neither of them had been trained to do this kind of
work. Noah had cautioned him against pursuing this, but
Gavin wasn't giving up just yet. If those bullets had been
meant to scare him, they had not succeeded. A new determination made him want to do his job.

Fifteen minutes later, traffic started moving again and
Gavin drove to headquarters, parked, then opened the back
to let Tommy out of the vehicle. Together they headed for
the indoor practice area like they'd done a thousand times
before. As he gave Tommy some playtime, he wondered
what Bree was doing. He didn't see her or Stella in the
training arena. A few minutes later, his phone buzzed.

Brianne.

She'd said she wanted to know more and that she wanted
to help him. Did Brianne Hayes really care at all?

He hit Accept and waited to see, torn between needing
her help and wanting to protect her.

"Gavin, meet me in the small conference room upstairs," she said, her words breathless. "We got a call
from the FBI. We might have a lead on the Fourth of July
bomber."

"I'll be right there."

Gavin put away his phone and forgot about his damp
uniform.

He wanted to see if they'd found the man in the park.

Because he felt pretty sure the man who'd placed bombs
in the East River Park could also be the same bomber
who'd been setting off small explosions for the past few
months. First thing, he'd report his suspicions to Noah.
This case had taken another turn and since several law

enforcement agencies were involved, he wanted full transparency. No mistakes.

They might have found the elusive man everyone on the streets called the Tick. The man knew they'd seen him last night. If the Tick had reported seeing them to whoever was paying him, then Gavin felt sure he'd been made and the Tick's boss had sent someone to rattle him this morning.

Did he dare bring Brianne into that kind of trap?

FIVE

Brianne watched Gavin making his way through the rows of cubicles where most of the K-9 Unit members did their desk work. The chief's office took up most of the back of the big room, its glass windows covered with blinds near a small anteroom where his assistant, Sophie, sat as gate-keeper. The other half of the office space there went to other supervisors and held smaller offices on each side. The conference room filled out the rest of the back part of this top floor. A training arena downstairs gave the K-9s a place to work out and practice mandatory train-ing all year long.

Gavin nodded to several officers but kept walking, Tommy at his side, until he reached the conference room. "What have we got?" he asked without so much as a nod.

She still wore her soggy uniform since she'd hurried up to do a database search of the man they'd seen last night, hoping she might remember something about the shoot-ing this morning in the process.

Gavin looked impatient. "Well?"

The man took his work seriously.

"For now, mug shots," she said, turning to head to the conference table where a photo she'd printed lay on the table. "One of the images I found looks like the man we saw in the park. A younger version from what I can tell. I sent it to the FBI right away and they called just now. They talked to a witness and that witness remembered seeing the man in the plaid cap. They sent the photo to the witness to verify. She says it could be the same man because of the shaggy hair. But she's not sure."

"Then that won't help us." Gavin stared at the photo of a dark-haired man with brown eyes and heavy brows. "Caucasian and about the same height and weight of our suspect but younger, yes. I don't know. He had on shades part of the time. Hard to say."

He sank down, exhaustion clear in his eyes. "My CI heard two men talking near an older apartment building in Midtown. Beanpole lives on the streets in that area and because he's basically invisible, people stand by where he sits on a corner and talk about all kinds of things. He says the bomber named the Tick is working on something big in Manhattan."

"Well, maybe your CI can ID him, too." She handed him the mug shot.

Gavin stared at the picture. "William Caston? How'd he wind up in the AFIS database?"

"Arrested seven years ago for being with a group of college kids who were setting off pipe bombs in Queens," Brianne said. "But he only got a few years of probation because another kid confessed to setting up the whole operation."

"Maybe the Tick decided to try a better bomb-making career," Gavin said. "I can't be sure if this is him."

She stared at the photo. "That would put his age at around thirty-one. It sounds like the the Tick is around that age, based on what little information I've managed to dig up."

"True, but we can't go on that alone."

"I got up close," Brianne said, hoping he wouldn't make a scene because she'd beat him to the punch. "I saw his face and though he wore sunglasses and that hat, I remember the shape of his face and his hair—scraggly and dark. And those eyebrows."

"Do we have a last known address?"

"No. The FBI says he's always moving."

He stared at the picture. "We keep searching and when we hear from the lab, we can go after him."

"We could leak this picture to the press," she suggested, her voice low.

"Not yet. I'll find Beanpole and see if he can ID this man. If he's sober, that is."

"I've talked to the techs," she said, accepting his decision. "They've got the detonated bomb fragments unpacked and they set up an examination plan. They're taking high-def photos of everything they found and they're going over the fragments from the explosion, piece by piece. But that could take a while. They'll go over every inch of any fragment found on that bomb site and take their time puttingthings together."

"Like weeks." He nodded, fatigue cloaking his face. "Okay. Ilana Hawkins will work with the FBI and CSI to figure it out. She's the best forensic tech we have, and the lab team can discover even the most minute clues. Meantime, I'm going to go back over the Tick's file and see if I can find any markers that might match whatever they find."

Brianne stared up at him. "Do you think they could be the same man?"

"I don't know yet," he replied. "But Tommy picked up on something on that guy in the park and I'm thinking it was more than just the bomb. Like Tommy recognized his signature from another time, which means it could easily boil down to fibers or some sort of scent unique to this person or his clothes."

"Stella alerted, too. Which means her bomb-detection training is paying off."

Gavin didn't argue with that. "Chief Jameson will need

a lot of evidence to make a case, but my gut tells me the Fourth of July bomber could also be the Tick."

"Why would the Tick veer off to the park?" Brianne asked, her mind going to places she didn't want to see.

"That's the burning question," Gavin said. "Let's go talk to Noah and explain what we know for now. Then we'll talk to him about this other case."

Brianne nodded and then said, "Hey, go have a shower first. Put on your sweats, and I'll send your uniform out to be cleaned. Then I'll meet you back here."

Gavin actually smiled at that, "You might make a good wife yet," he deadpanned with a grin.

Bristling, she replied, "I don't intend to stay home wearing an apron, Sutherland, so let's get something straight. If I play the part of your wife, I'm going to be a pampered socialite who always gets her way. Don't expect me to cook and clean for you or pick up your dirty clothes."

"But you're willing to help with my dry cleaning?"

"That's easy. I just get on the phone and call someone. Mine needs cleaning, too."

"It's a start," he said. "I think I'll have that shower and then find some of that battery acid we call coffee. Thanks, Bree."

She smiled and watched him head toward the downstairs locker rooms, her mind whirling between cooking and cleaning or running behind a K-9 partner. She preferred the latter.

But she sure wouldn't mind spending some downtime with tall, stubborn and hard-to-read Gavin Sutherland.

Gavin got dressed as quickly as possible, then went back into the training arena to get Tommy. When he saw Tommy curled up in his kennel, he decided to leave his partner there for a few minutes. The springer worked hard and rarely complained.

Gavin called to one of the handlers. "I'm letting Tommy rest a while, okay?"

The handler nodded. "You both need to rest after last night—and this morning."

Gavin agreed with that, but he was too wired to stay still. That park bombing smacked of a setup, as did the shooting, but he needed more to go on before he went to Chief Noah Jameson with his conspiracy theory. They were getting back on an even footing and he did not want to mess that up. Noah liked solid evidence. They all did. He intended to find that evidence.

When he got back upstairs, he went straight to the conference room, surprised to see Brianne had already set up a white board with all the details of last night's bombing. The woman thrived on being knee-deep in any case.

Gavin studied the mug shot of the man Brianne believed to be the suspect. He'd never seen a photo of the Tick since the man always wore black, mostly hoodies, kept his face away from cameras and disguised himself with beards and mustaches, sometimes in different colors. But the eyebrows here were interesting. Real or fake? Hard to say.

Brianne came in with coffee and two big peach Danishes. "Food, Gavin. Eat."

He sat down and rubbed his eyes. "Man, I'm beat."

"I know. Me, too."

She sure didn't look tired with her neat and tidy hair off her face in a tight bun. She wore very little makeup, so he could enjoy the smattering of freckles tossed like sparkled dust across her cheeks and nose. And those eyes—a deep, rich brown that reminded him of the ancient trees up in the Poconos. She had the eyes of an old soul, full of determination and stubbornness, defiance and acceptance.

Nothing got past this woman. He'd be wise to remember that and he'd be wise to heed the warning bells in his head. They worked together. Nothing more.

"Hey," Brianne said. "Are you okay?"

Gavin blinked. Had he been staring? "Just putting things together in my head."

Things like walking in an old forest with her, holding her hand, kissing her.

Whoa on that. "It's just nagging me." *True.*

She was nagging him. Being so involved with her and this case—nagging him. Asking her to help him with the other case—nagging him big time. Because he'd given her an in and she wouldn't back down.

"You mean, because now we're dealing with two different bombers or that they could both be the same person?"

"Yeah, that."

"Something else?" She stood, daring him to dispute her.

"You, Bree."

"Me? What have I done? Are you mad that I jumped right into this? Isn't that what we're supposed to do? Are you like all the others, Gavin?"

"If you mean against women officers, no." He shook his head and smiled. "Are you finished?"

"I'm just getting started. I can't believe—"

"Relax, will you?" he said before he bit into the sugar-coated Danish. "You haven't done anything wrong. You've done everything right. I need someone to help me with this—I've been obsessed with the Tick since I realized he had to have been the one who set off a bomb in the Williamsburg building and all the others, too, for that matter."

"So what's your problem?"

"I don't have a problem. Other than Tommy, I'm not used to a partner."

"You asked me to help. Are you saying you don't work well with humans?"

"I'm fine with humans and yes, I did ask you to help, but I don't want to put you in unnecessary danger."

"That's my job. Is this about me being a woman?"

"Do people still discriminate like that?" he asked, meaning it. "That did not enter my mind, other than noticing that you are definitely a woman."

She stopped, staring at him in a new way that almost scared him. "Oh, I get it. You like me? Right? I mean, you did ask me to go for coffee? Just a friendly thing? Are you flirting with me, Gavin? Is that it? I scare you and you don't want to get involved with a coworker, so you're telling me I'm a problem?"

"That's not what I meant." But she was close. He didn't need a work-time romance. Other such notions had taught him to never cross that line, especially now when he'd just been through too much scrutiny already. Romancing a coworker wasn't wise.

Brianne sat down across from him and attacked her Danish. "First, we *are* working together, so get over the notion that anything else can happen between us." Chewing with determination she stared him down. "And second, this is a juicy case. I know we're on the task force to find Chief Jameson's killer and I'm all over that one, too. But bomb detection is our thing. You and me. Our thing. So I'm in now, Gavin. Unless the chief tells us otherwise. Got it?"

Gavin took it all in. Her magnificent display of letting him have it with both barrels only reinforced that he was in over his head with her. "Yeah, that," he said, wishing he'd kept his mouth shut on asking her to be in on it.

"Oh, I get it. You're regretting asking me, right?"

"Just a tad."

"Gavin, get over yourself. Are we doing this or not?"

"We're doing it," he said, grudgingly. "I need your help and upon further thinking, I'd say you're perfect for the job."

"I do watch a lot of those home-buying shows—you know the ones on the channel that shows people searching for the perfect house. And another show that's all about New York real estate. I can play the part. I just need a designer purse and some kicking shoes and makeup and a fancy car and a big wallet."

"The chief will flip over that budget."

"Go big or go home," she quipped. "I have connections. I think I can pull that part off. Let's go lay out the case for him." Then she gave him that stare of steel. "And, Gavin, I mean the whole case. We have to tell him we think all of this could be the work of one man."

Gavin finished his Danish and coffee, his mind boiling with the hows and whys of these two cases. He needed to talk to Noah. Couldn't leave anything to chance with such a dangerous man setting off bombs all over New York City.

"Let me gather my files and links," he said, admiration for Brianne's spunk giving him hope. He'd either become a better man for having her on his side or she'd do him in, piece by piece.

But for now, he had to trust her.

He needed a fake wife.

The interim chief stared at both of them as if they'd changed into two-headed monsters. "Are you serious?"

"Very," Gavin said, gearing up for a battle. "You know I've been working this case for months and I've contributed to trying to find Jordan's murderer, too. But this is getting out of hand, sir. I need Officer Hayes to assist me with this undercover operation."

"Why Officer Hayes?" Noah asked, his no-nonsense expression intimidating, his green eyes full of doubt.

Gavin refused to be intimidated, however. "She's a good officer, she's trained in bomb detection and she's training Stella—the dog that first picked up the Fourth of July bomber's scent."

"I have the facts, Sutherland," Noah said, his gaze moving between them. "But why do you need a partner now?"

Brianne sat up. "Sir, we think we'd get farther as a couple. It looks more believable and...two sets of eyes are always better than one."

Noah positioned his stare on Brianne. "And you're willing to do this? Put yourself at risk?"

"I put myself at risk every day, sir," she replied, cool as mint-infused lemonade. "This is no different. I stared into that bomber's face. I agree with Gavin. This could be the same man."

"I'm not buying that," Noah replied, shaking his head. "Coincidence. This is a big city with a hundred threats a day. Threats that we contain while people go about their business, never knowing what we've done."

"We don't think it was coincidence," Gavin replied, aggravated that his superior couldn't trust him. "But until we hear back from the crime lab, we have to go on the assumption that the Tick will strike again. You know how brutal the real estate business is, sir. Especially in Manhattan. We can't risk someone else getting hurt or killed."

Noah leaned back in his chair, his frown weary with fatigue. "And what about finding my brother's killer?"

"We'll continue to do what needs to be done on that," Gavin assured him. "For as long as it takes."

Noah sat silent for a minute. A very long minute.

"All right. This is highly irregular because K-9 officers don't usually go undercover, but using the dogs while you make a few inquiries can't hurt. Just play it safe and don't get too involved in going deep." Waving his hands at them, he added, "Fill out the proper papers on what you need and watch the cost because we don't have much of a budget. Keep me updated and…Gavin, be careful."

Gavin nodded and stood. "Thanks. We'll get this figured out."

"I hope so," Noah replied. Then he looked Gavin in the eye. "I wasn't sure about taking this job and I'm still not sure. I'm trying to do my best. I know we put you through the wringer but…he was my brother. No stone unturned, even when it meant interrogating you."

"I agree," Gavin said, taking the apology as a good sign. "No stone unturned. You have my word on that. If you get any leads, send them to us, sir."

They left Noah's office in silence and didn't speak again until they were outside.

Then Brianne turned to him and gave him an appreciative smile. "You are one tough cop, Gavin."

"Right back at you."

She started for her car, Stella trailing along. "I guess we start fresh tomorrow, right?"

He nodded. "I'll call the next agent on my real estate list and set up a showing with him. He mentioned some apartment buildings in Midtown and the Upper West Side. I'll ask him to show us one of those to begin with and we'll work our way toward a targeted building. Might take a couple of days."

"Meantime, we can do what needs to be done on Jordan's case."

"Good plan."

Then she asked, "How are we going to coordinate this undercover thing?"

He stopped with her near where their cars were parked.

"There's a safe house I've been using in Midtown whenever I'm in Manhattan on this case. Approved from the top for certain cases." He gave her the address of a boutique hotel on a quiet side street. "Suite 305. I'll pick you up there each time we're on this case. Be dressed and ready to play your part."

"As your wife," she said, her eyes holding his. "Linus and Alice Reinhart. Catchy names, by the way."

He'd discussed their cover with her earlier.

"Yes, as my wife." Then, because he wanted to get a rise out of her, he added, "But please don't wear any aprons, okay?"

She threw it right back into his face. "No apron, I can assure you. Alice Reinhart doesn't wear aprons, darling."

Gavin couldn't stop his grin. "I can't wait."

He let Tommy into his SUV kennel and then watched as she did the same with Stella, his protective nature taking over.

Tomorrow, they began the real work. The dangerous work.

He prayed he'd be able to keep her safe.

SIX

Two days later, Gavin drove the rental car through the small portico in front of the Gable Hotel. The department used this discreet, out-of-the-way spot as a safe house as needed since it looked more like a Victorian house than a true hotel. The owners were also discreet, and the place had a top-notch security system to boot.

Gavin entered and waved to the desk clerk, then headed up to the assigned room and tapped on the door. "It's Gavin and Tommy."

They'd both agreed to let Stella continue training with another handler for a few days while they used Tommy as Brianne's companion dog. So it would be strange seeing her without Stella at her side. Also it would be a shock to see her out of uniform and actually dressed in civilian clothes.

All of that went out of Gavin's head as he stared at the woman who opened the door and then stood back.

Brianne Hayes sure cleaned up nicely.

She wore her hair swept up in a way that probably required technique but looked like she'd just tossed it together with a big clip. And it looked darker. She wore a red dress. Red with just enough sleeve to be demure and a flowing skirt that showed off her waist before it flowed down to her knees. Pearls coiled around her neck and her shoes were tall with lots of black straps. The purse had some famous designer's initials all over it and shouted money.

"Hi," she said. Then she leaned down and patted Tommy's wiry spotted fur before wrapping a sparkling rhinestone and black leather dog collar around his neck.

"So he looks the part," she said with a shrug and a smile.

Tommy shot Gavin a helpless look but didn't move a muscle. The K-9 was nothing if not professional, but this? *Seriously*?

"Seriously," Gavin replied to Tommy's perplexed stare. Yes, he and Tommy were so used to talking back and forth they could read each other's expressions.

"Doesn't he look like a pampered pooch?" Brianne asked, eying the sparkling leather collar. "I tried to find one that looked mannish."

"Oh, he looks mannish all right," Gavin said, wondering if his suit came off expensive enough to make him look mannish. And he was still stunned by just watching her walk toward him in those shoes and that dress. Giving Tommy a brush of assurance, he whispered, "Don't worry, buddy. A brand new tennis ball is in your future."

She stood and adjusted her purse, a whiff of some sweet, exotic scent flowing around her. "Ready?"

"I don't know. How do *I* look?" he asked, unable to get anything else to come out of his mouth.

"Good," she said in a tone that showed she meant it. "The mustache matches your eyes."

"What did you do to your hair?" he asked, hoping it wasn't permanent.

"Temporary dye. It'll wash out."

Having solved that mystery, he got down to business.

"Did getting here go okay?" he asked as they stepped down the winding staircase to the first floor.

Nodding again to the front desk clerk, Gavin led her out

onto the steps of the old brownstone where they both did a scan of the surrounding quiet tree-shaded street.

"I got up early and took the subway in from headquarters—checked that I wasn't being tailed—and then flashed my badge to the desk clerk, as you instructed. She took me right up to the suite and I spent most of the morning pampering myself and getting ready. This place is nice in an old-fashioned way. I left my stuff here so I need to come back later today, but I do have the room overnight if needed."

Glad to hear no one followed her, Gavin took her arm and escorted her down the steps. At first, she frowned at his gesture. "For show," he quickly explained while he ignored the soft skin that felt warm against his callused fingers.

"Oh, okay then." She took in the car. "Fancy sedan? Did the chief approve this?"

"He did, grudgingly," Gavin admitted, his gaze moving over the sleek gray car before he checked the street. "But it takes money to make money and in this case, it takes a fancy car to flush out corrupt people. Besides, I know a guy who knows a guy at the rental company. I got the friends-and-family rate."

He opened the door for her, causing her to frown. "Part of the cover," he said to hide the fact that he enjoyed doing it. "A gentleman always takes care of his lady."

Brianne gave him a perplexed glance and then let Tommy onto the backseat. Turning, she slid into the car, her actions as prim as any socialite's.

"You sure look nice," he said.

"Just part of the cover," she mimicked, a teasing twinkle in her eyes.

She enjoyed tormenting him!

The woman might be all business on the surface but

underneath she was a scamp. Making him squirm while he tried to stay focused.

"You're enjoying this too much," he said. "But I am getting to know the real you."

"You don't know the real me," she said, her tone serious now. "And since I'm wearing borrowed clothes and makeup that costs more than a week's salary, you have to know this kind of getup is so not me."

"Is it okay if I get to know you?" he replied, treading that line between being professional and falling at her feet in surrender.

"I'm good with that," she said. "But right now, we need to go over our cover material. You know the real estate agents will do a thorough background check on us so they can drool over our assets."

"All taken care of," he said to get back on track. "Since I set up my own background months ago, and some of them know I've been single, I went back and added you as my new bride. We met in the Hamptons and fell in love, had a whirlwind marriage and honeymooned in Europe. Now we need a place to live in Manhattan."

"Do I work?"

"Not anymore, darling."

"What if I have a career and I'm a highly independent woman?"

"We can go with that, too."

"And what do you do, Linus, my new husband?"

Loving the way that sounded on her lips, he said, "I'm an entrepreneur who dabbles in real estate investments on a big scale. So we'll look at the penthouse, but we'd like to buy an older building and tear it down. Progress, of course. We need to drop that into the conversation, by the way."

"Perfect. So we're covered there."

"Solid. Danielle and our other techs enjoyed setting this one up for us."

Brianne scanned the road ahead. "Dani is like a fairy godmother and with her curly blond hair and all the bling she wears, she would know. She gave me some great fashion tips and she knows this guy who sells purses. Don't ask."

Gavin silently thanked their eclectic tech analyst, yet again. Then he got down to business. "The park bombing concerns me in more ways than one. What if I've been made already? What if we're walking into a trap?"

"We have to make *them* believe *us*, Gavin," she said. "And if it is a trap, then we find a way to get out and bring them down."

"You shouldn't sound so bold and brave."

"We both look completely different today than we did at the park the other night. Even if the bomber noticed us, we were in uniform with patrol hats covering most of our hair. And today, we won't come face-to-face with the alleged bomber, right?"

"I sure hope not. Not yet, anyway. I want to get to the person hiring the man."

Brianne watched the road and kept looking around at the interior of the car. "We have to be bold and brave. It's our job. So don't make it sound like you're not the same way. I've seen you in action. I can take care of myself, but I'm also going to watch out for you. You'd do the same for me."

He couldn't argue with her spot-on logic. "Okay, but if things get out of hand, promise you'll be careful."

"I'm always careful," she replied.

He worried she liked this stuff too much. She was good at her job, yes, but the adrenaline rush could take over sometimes. She could become reckless. He prayed against that. He wasn't reckless. Maybe that's why he got passed up for promotions. He wasn't scared of taking matters into his own hands, but Granny Irene had taught him to be thorough and always do what was right. While Brianne seemed to have those same values, he knew this job could go to a person's head, too. Or mess with a person's head. One slip and it would all be over.

"Bree, I mean it. This is dangerous work."

"I know that," she said. "I'm not so careless that I'd put myself or you and Tommy in danger. I've done my home-work. I memorized your files on this case and I've done some research on my own. These people target buildings in transition, the kind that need a quick sell. Explosions can bring that about easily enough." Then she shrugged. "This is New York. For someone with a lot of money, any-thing is possible. Buyouts are common here but then so is corruption."

"Okay then." Impressed, he shifted the car and headed through the Manhattan traffic, his heart tripping over it-self while he hoped he wouldn't regret this. They had a part to play, but he preferred real life.

And maybe way down the road, a date so he could relax with the real Brianne Hayes.

As they got closer to the property, he said, "This is the Sherriman Building, owned by Sherriman Properties. Our real estate agent is Justin Sanelli from the Rexx Agency, a hotshot playboy who brags about getting the best deals in town. If a seller won't come down on the price, Justin makes it happen. He is the big dog at Rexx and has about twenty agents under him."

"So he's not first on our list. I read in your report you'd already ruled out three others since they didn't fit the mode."

"No, he's number four. He might not be the last, but he

got on my radar after I met him at an open house. I did some research on him but couldn't pin anything to him. After attending business school and getting his real estate license, he hired on with a small agency in Chelsea and worked his way up. Now he travels in high-up circles and works the room with his charm."

"I'm guessing his persuasive tactics are enlightening," she said, "in a booming way."

"That's what I think. Just as you said, his firm swoops in when a building is in trouble, buys out the frustrated person or company holding the deed to the entire property or pushes the owners out. Then Sanelli gets a good deal and a prime piece of real estate, touting that he *rescues* distressed properties and flips them to make them million-dollar investments."

"I can't believe someone hasn't noticed this pattern before."

"Think about it," Gavin said as he maneuvered the smooth-riding car through the stop-and-go traffic. "All the buildings for sale in New York and accidents happening every day—easy to let something like this slip right on by. We got a break with that explosion in Williamsburg when Tommy picked up on what remained of the bomb. Before that, we were just working with what looked like a boiler explosion in the maintenance room. Now that scent is embedded in his system. The Tick isn't careless, but something went wrong there and he left us just a trace of his bomb-making DNA. And now I'm onto him."

"And if he's also the Fourth of July bomber, Tommy and Stella both have his number, too."

When they arrived at the building, Brianne stared up the redbrick structure trimmed in white stone and intricate molding. "It's not as tall as most."

"No, just fifteen floors, but exclusive. Prewar at its

best with those tall ceilings, big rooms and solid walls. We're looking at the penthouse—three bedrooms and three baths—and many millions of dollars. It used to be four apartments, but someone had a big family and combined all of them."

"Who has that kind of money?"

"It's passed hands several times and been renovated. The original owners made a pretty penny when they sold it about five years ago. But the rest of the building needs a lot of work."

"So Justin sees an opportunity here."

"Yes. The company that owns the building is holding out for a high price, but Justin assures me he can get them down. So first we focus on the penthouse and then we tell him we'd like to buy the entire building."

"Yeah, right," she said. "Why do people have to be so greedy? He'll get the current owner to come down but then he'll still make a profit because he'll turn around and broker the whole building."

"Especially if he blows up part of the building and sends down the property value because of structural problems. The current residents will be so ready to sell, one by one. The Tick thrives on being a domestic terrorist."

Gavin shot Brianne one last look as he pulled the car up to the curb in front of the complex with its adjacent garage and gave his name to the valet attendant. "Linus and Alice Reinhart, here to see Justin Sanelli."

The dour guard at the door gave them and their vehicle a once-over and nodded to the young valet. They were in.

There would be no turning back after this.

Once they were out of the car, the burly guard studied them and then sent a text upward. "Go ahead," he finally said after getting a reply, seemingly bored with all of it.

After the valet took the car, they made their way to the spacious lobby where a fountain gurgled and soft music played. The place looked rundown but held a patina of elegance. Another guard behind the rounded desk nodded and walked with them to the elevator. He, too, eyed them in a money-hungry but bored way. "Mr. Sanelli is on his way down."

"Fancy," Brianne whispered, hoping her eyes didn't pop out of her head. She tried to look as bored as the guards they'd just encountered, but her heart raced and she couldn't stop the awe in seeing such a historic and expensive building. "Very art deco."

Tommy did his part. He sniffed as any dog would but stayed near her since she held his leash. She had to control herself or the K-9 would pick up on her nervous energy. But Tommy knew all the tricks of the trade and he could handle a fake out same as they could.

Gavin kept his voice low. "Sanelli's meeting us here because, as I mentioned, a while back I encountered him at an open house in another building similar to this one. After we'd talked a while, I explained what I was looking for."

Gavin had told her earlier that Justin had hinted about his unique ways of getting stubborn sellers to cave and agree to any offers. *He has ways*, Gavin now reaffirmed. Business was booming.

Gavin had honed in on Sanelli, his gut telling him this might be their man. "I've been watching him for weeks but nothing out of the ordinary. He's a hustler but I can't pin anything definite on him."

"Ah, the setup," she replied, her smile serene as they waited for Justin to come down and escort them to the top of the building. "I'll pretend I'm interested in the whole building. I mean, only the best for my sweet boy."

Gavin rolled his eyes. "You'd buy a building just to please your dog?"

The elevator dinged, and she went into full-on fake mode.

"Linus, you know T-Boy is more than a dog," she said, her voice rising as she stared over at him. "T-Boy is my companion, a sure comfort when you leave me alone and go off on yet another scouting-for-real-estate trip."

Gavin obviously figured their man would be interested and went with it. "Alice, I have to travel for work, darling. But if you think buying a building will make you and T-Boy happy, then that's what we'll do. And I'll try to find more business ventures in the city so I can stay home with you more."

Alice sent him an air-kiss and then giggled, pushing past him to the average-looking man standing behind Gavin. "You must be Justin. Did you hear us bickering?"

Justin Sanelli laughed and gently shook her hand, his frosty blue eyes wide with obvious glee. "I call that negotiating," he chirped. "And if you're serious about wanting the entire building, I can work with you on that."

"Let's talk upstairs," Gavin said, shooting his wife an indulgent smile.

They got in the elevator with the blond-haired man who wore what looked like a tailor-made suit. Brianne watched the elevator stop on the P level. Penthouse.

Brianne winked at Gavin, her arm on his, her heart doing funny little skittish leaps. "This is an impressive building. I love the crown molding and the big windows."

Justin did an elaborate bow. "Then you're really going to love the penthouse." With a flourish, he opened the doors and stood back. "Best view in the city."

Brianne looked through the massive rooms and out into

the city beyond, her gaze moving past the buildings and toward the Hudson River.

Then she clapped her hands and giggled. "I can't wait to see the rest of this place."

Gavin gave her a brilliant fake smile.

But Brianne wished he'd really smile at her. He looked handsome in his nice suit, his dark hair shining and combed.

She might be living in a fantasy world right this minute, but her mind wandered beyond large apartments with beautiful views. She thought of a small fenced yard and dogs running along with children, dinner on the table and her man by her side. Why did she have to envision Gavin in that role?

Impossible.

"Let's go inside," Justin said, bursting her bubble.

Giggling again, she purred down to Tommy. "What do you think, T-Boy? Could this be our new home?"

The dog woofed, but she couldn't be sure if he agreed with her or if he was just disgusted. She was sure of one thing. Tommy had not alerted on the real estate broker, which meant he didn't have any trace of explosives on him today.

Gavin grinned and took her hand. When he squeezed it reassuringly, Brianne felt an explosion inside her heart.

An explosion every bit as scary and dangerous as the real thing. For the first time since she'd signed up for this mission, Brianne had to wonder if she'd made a huge mistake.

SEVEN

Justin Sanelli primed himself like a dancer trying to win a competition, full of superlatives and over-the-top bragging rights. "We grossed close to half-a-billion dollars last year and we should surpass that this year. I have an outstanding team, fabulous and ruthless. We get properties moving."

"Thank you for personally meeting us here," Gavin said, his expression showing pretend-fatigue. "We are certainly impressed."

Brianne went to the windows again to stare out at the view. Exposure to the north, south and east. Central Park wasn't that far from here and Fifth Avenue flowed just around the corner. There was a concierge, a doorman and those guards they'd endured…a fitness center and rooftop pool… Luxury. The way the sunshine shot through these big windows showed a different side of life. This sun highlighted beautiful furniture and expensive artwork, not the grit and grime she saw down there on the street. The deck—covered with wrought iron, cushioned furniture, thriving dish gardens and parlor palms that would have to be moved inside come winter—was bigger than the basement apartment she lived in.

Gavin came up behind her and put his arms around her. Brianne almost decked him and then remembered he was her pretend-husband. So, for just a moment, she leaned into the strength of his arms and enjoyed the view, her heart hurting for all of the people who didn't have this panoramic indulgence.

"What are you thinking, sweetheart?" he asked, his fingers covering her hands.

Brianne put away her thoughts, his endearments and went back to work. "I'm thinking I love this penthouse and I want this whole building." Then she turned and put on a good show for Justin Sanelli. "I mean, this is prime property. Think of what we could do if we tore this building down and started from scratch." Looking up into Gavin's questioning eyes, she touched her hand to his jaw and felt his pulse quicken. "Let's keep this one in mind but maybe we should tour a few more. I know we can afford this but… I also know how to negotiate."

"You are very good at negotiating and saving money is important," Gavin responded, his tone husky. "And yet I want to give you the world. Everything you've ever dreamed of."

Something in his words caught Brianne and held her, but the look in his dark eyes made her dream of that house in the suburbs again. The best view was the one you could treasure each and every day, a blessing, a home, a safe haven. She couldn't see that view here in this over-the-top fancy environment.

But she sure could see that view in Gavin's eyes.

Justin coughed, not wanting to miss this opportunity. "I can work on the owner. He's sentimental since his mother lived in this building until the day she died. And since you mentioned the whole building, I can make sellers see the light. Just name your price and we'll get everyone who's still left here to agree to your offer."

Gavin shot Brianne a warning glance. "We'll consider this one, Justin. But we'd like to look around over the next couple of weeks. I have a good feeling we'll be back, but we never buy the first thing we look at."

Justin hid his disappointment well. "I'll see what else I can find. So you're interested in the best for less, correct?"

"Correct, and we are very interested in buildings such as this one—the whole building," Gavin said, his eyes on Brianne. "Keep doing what you're doing and I'm sure we'll find a property that meets our needs very soon."

They left on good terms. Justin would shake down the whole of Manhattan to find them a bargain—one that would ultimately bring them all what they wanted.

And maybe bring jail time for the broker.

Brianne waited until they were back in the sleek sedan before she let out a breath. "If he is our man, he's going to have a very hard time adjusting to a jail cell."

"Yep." Gavin watched the traffic and kept checking the mirrors for any tails. "Tommy didn't alert on him, so I know he's not our possible bomber, but I had hoped for something to come out of this. I could be wrong all around."

"Well, he could be working for someone. Same as the Tick. We need to get to the big guy."

Gavin nodded and watched the road, concern clouding his handsome face.

Wondering why he remained so quiet, she tried again. "I'm starving. Let's find some food."

"We need to change first. Unless you want me to take you to a restaurant I really can't afford."

"We can change at the safe house," she suggested. "Then I want to go home. I'll take the subway back to get my vehicle from headquarters."

"I'll take you after we change and eat."

"No, I don't expect that," she replied, thinking she could just eat at home by herself. Then she went on without thinking. "I live with my parents, but they're visiting my aunt and uncle out on Long Island for a few weeks. We can order a pizza and unwind at my house."

Gavin gave her a panicked glance. "Uh, I don't know..."

From the look on his face, he obviously didn't like that idea. "I mean, I guess we could do that but—"

"Okay then, forget it. I'm beat and I can't wait to get out of these clothes."

"I could go for pizza," he finally said. "I'm trying to figure out the logistics. I have to hide our fancy car in a secure parking garage that has excellent surveillance. My vehicle is parked around from where I need to leave our rented car."

Relaxing, she understood his hesitation. "You don't want to blow your cover."

"Right."

"Sure, you can give me a ride to headquarters. Makes sense. I'm dying to ditch this dress—it's a loaner so I can't keep it. At least I can bring Stella home with me if we swing by headquarters."

"Too bad you can't keep the dress," he said and then looked sheepish. "I mean, it's nice."

"Nice? Danielle borrowed it from a sample sale at Saks. She knows people there. This is more than nice. It's an original—a designer dress."

"I should have said that it's a knockout dress and I can tell by the cut and the thread that it's worth *every* dollar—several hundred—someone might spend to buy it."

"That's better."

Sending her an appreciative glance, he asked, "Are you sure you don't want to walk through the training yard to get Stella wearing that outfit?"

That made her laugh. "I'm not going anywhere near the training arena until I've changed. Do you want to eat pizza at my house or not, 'cause I'm ordering one with or without you, Sutherland."

He studied her and then nodded. "I'm in."

"Change first. Garage second. Headquarters third. Pizza at my house—finally."

"That's a good plan, Bree," he said. "We have to be careful with this whole operation."

"Then let's take the long way back to the garage," she suggested. "Just in case."

Gavin nodded and meandered through the city to switch cars. Careful, they made their way out of the garage on foot and headed toward his official SUV. The sun began to descend behind the buildings to the west and the streets filled with commuters on their way home from work.

Why did the night seem so sinister? The heat sizzled over the asphalt and concrete in hot waves.

"So far, so good." His relief was obvious after they were in his vehicle and going through the Queens–Midtown Tunnel. "I don't think anyone followed us," he said an hour later. They turned toward the K-9 Unit building. "We can meet back at our vehicles after you get Stella. I'll follow you to your house."

"Okay, it's not too far from headquarters," she replied. "I live in Corona."

"Will you be safe?"

Wondering why he worried so much, Brianne stiffened her spine. "Gavin, seriously? I'll see you back here and i'll have Stella with me. We'll meet at my house for pizza."

Once they entered the lobby, Brianne kept her head up and took the stairs down to the training arena, the sound of her sturdy heels clicking an echo that sounded too loud in her ears. Taking a quick shower in the women's locker room where she'd stashed her clothes earlier, she rinsed the dark color out of her hair.

Being a rich wife had zapped her.

The locker room looked empty so she hurried to her locker and made sure she had everything in order before she left for the day. Then she ran a hand through her hair and twisted it up into a damp bun.

"Free," she said, hurrying to find Stella. When she ran into Noah Jameson near the stairs, she nodded. "Sir."

His gaze swept over her. "How did it go, Officer Hayes? Give me a report."

She didn't want to steal Gavin's thunder, but her superior had asked her a direct question. "We made contact with a man who could be one of our suspects." She went on to explain Justin Sanelli. "But this is just the beginning. It's possible he's hiring the Tick to make things happen."

"I sure hope we find that bomber," Noah said. "You're both going out on a limb here and this is highly unusual. But I'm learning sometimes we have to bend the rules to find justice."

Brianne worried about their interim chief. Noah wanted justice for his brother, Jordan. Would his grief cause him to do whatever it took, no matter the cost? She'd said a lot of prayers for the three remaining Jameson brothers. They were tough but sooner or later the grief could cave in. "Yes, sir, but we'll stay within the rules so we don't mess up."

Noah nodded, and then he gave her a twisted smile. "You sure seem to be in a hurry to get home. Long day?"

Embarrassed, she lowered her head. "Uh…you saw me coming in?"

"I see everyone who comes and goes," Noah replied. "Just be careful. We've all been dealing with a lot lately."

"Yes, sir, I plan to stay alert. And Gavin's got my back."

"I hope so," the chief replied. "I'm counting on it."

Now she could see why this case meant so much to Gavin. He still had a lot to prove to the Jameson brothers.

Her heart hurt, knowing he had no one to turn to.

That's wrong, she thought. *He has me now. And I've got his back, too.* She didn't know when she'd come to that conclusion but…she wouldn't let Gavin down. She'd start a new prayer thread for Gavin—asking the Lord to protect her temporary partner.

After checking her phone for any messages—one from her mom telling her they were having fun and reminding her to stay safe, but nothing else much—Brianne followed the chief to the K-9 training area. She saw Gavin standing with Tommy, talking to Carter Jameson. Of all the brothers, Carter reached out to Gavin the most. They seemed close again, at least.

She nodded at them and after chatting with the chief a while, went to find Stella. Rookie K-9 Officer Lani Branson greeted her. "Hey, we need to have another girls night soon. I sure could use one."

"I need that, too," Brianne answered as she walked toward her friend and saw Stella running toward them from the kennel area. "It's been crazy lately, but I'll try to squeeze one in soon."

Lani, blonde, buff and so New York, looked more like a model than an officer of the law. She handed off Stella to Brianne, her graceful and easy moves reminding Brianne she'd once been an actor and a dancer. But she'd given that up, taught self-defense classes and then decided to become a K-9 officer. Talk about a career turnaround.

"Heard you're on a job with Gavin Sutherland," Lani said with a knowing grin. "How's that going?"

Not wanting to give too much away since the unit members assumed they were working on Jordan's case and the bombing in the park, Brianne said, "It's interesting. A little nerve-wracking."

Lani gave her an unabashed stare. "I'm thinking you'll be good for Gavin. He's intense."

"He can be," Brianne admitted. "But then so can I. We're working through it."

She'd heard rumors that the chief and Gavin had once been friends and Gavin had confirmed that. But something had happened years ago to drive them apart. An argument about how to conduct a training session had come between them, but Brianne didn't plan on trying to get the details out of Gavin until he wanted to talk.

Maybe Brianne could get Gavin to open up about that. Maybe over pizza or, if not, then later when he trusted her more. She'd suggested a meal and some down time so she could get a better read on the man. She liked knowing she could trust a person and so far she trusted Gavin. But she wanted him to trust her and not worry about her. She could handle this.

Well, she could handle the case and the danger.

Her erratic feelings regarding her temporary partner? Another matter altogether. She'd have to keep a close watch over her heart with this one.

"Hey, you okay?" Lani asked. "Is Gavin already giving you grief?"

"You could say that, but this is only a temporary partnership, so I'll be okay."

Lani discreetly dropped the subject of Gavin and gave Stella a parting pat. "We had a good workout today. She found bomb materials we'd planted in the locker room and out in the training yard. This girl definitely has a nose for explosives."

"Good to know," Brianne said, pleased. "Ready to go home, Miss Stella?"

Stella danced around to give Lani a goodbye smile. Then she looked up at Brianne for further instructions.

Laughing, Brianne said, "Let's go then."

Brianne took her leash, noting she wore a black training vest to get her acclimated to wearing a bulletproof vest later. "Dinner soon, Lani. And we'll invite Faith, too." The single mom, also a K-9 officer, had a cute four-year-old named Jane. She could always use a break.

"That's a plan," Lani said, her gaze moving from Brianne to where Gavin and Carter stood. "I think Gavin's been waiting for you."

Brianne didn't tell her friend she was having pizza with Gavin Sutherland. Lani would jump to the wrong conclusion. So she just waved and headed toward Gavin and Carter. And noticed the chief hurrying back upstairs, walking right past the too-curious Lani without a word.

Gavin walked with her out to her vehicle and did a thorough scan of the surrounding area.

Brianne did the same. Someone could be watching them right now. Ignoring that feeling, she said, "I'll pick up the pizza. You have my address, right?"

"Got it," he said, his gaze moving back and forth. "You should take Tommy with you, too."

"I have Stella. She can bark, you know."

"I know that but… Tommy is a seasoned K-9."

"Gavin, stop it. If you keep this up, you'll have me changing my mind. You have to trust me to do my job."

"I can't help it. This is dangerous, and I shouldn't have dragged you into it."

"Well, too late to worry about that." Cutting him some slack, she added, "My dad bought an alarm a couple of years ago. And Stella and I like quiet time when we first get home. Girl talk and all."

"So you can talk about me?" he quipped.

Tommy's ears lifted. "See, Tommy wants to hear, too."

"Of course. He's probably wondering why you and I were so lovey-dovey earlier."

The shrewd dog looked from him to Brianne, his tongue hanging out in what could only be described as a smile.

Gavin watched as she let Stella into the kennel and then turned to open the SUV door. "I'll lay off but…be careful."

"Always. I'll see you soon, with pizza—one pepperoni and one veggie."

He walked backward to his vehicle. "Don't eat all of the pepperoni before I get there."

A bit later, Brianne had the pizza and drove home, keeping an eye on any vehicles behind her. But no one turned off to follow her up her street. Careful when she got out, she once again did a scan of the quiet area and saw nothing out of the ordinary. So she opened the door and turned on the lights.

"Search," she told Stella, to test the newbie and to reassure herself. Stella took off, glad to have a command but came back to stare up at her. "What's wrong?" Brianne asked, her heart rate accelerating. Placing the pizza on the counter, she tugged at her gun holster. "Search," she said again, moving behind Stella through the empty house.

Stella took her downstairs, to the door that opened from her basement apartment to the backyard. Not waiting, Brianne opened the back door, noticed the motion detector light was on and sent Stella out. "Find."

Stella took off.

Brianne thought she heard a noise out by the back fence but before she could check it out, the doorbell rang upstairs.

She jumped.

Stella barked.

Another noise, shuffling and then footsteps running away.

Brianne started out the back door but the bell rang again. Should she go after the intruder or shout out to Gavin? Hurrying since she didn't even have her phone, she held her gun in front of her and used the security light to check the backyard. Nothing.

But Stella sat by the far fence, a soft growl emitting from the dog's throat. Someone had been here and left, probably hopping over the fence. But the outside door to her apartment was intact. No damage.

Maybe Gavin was wise to be so cautious, she decided.

But she couldn't let him see her doubts or fears.

She had to stay strong and alert because Gavin wasn't the only one who had something to prove. Her focus had to remain on two things—finding that bomber and finding Jordan Jameson's killer.

There could be no room for a third in there. Even a good-looking third named Gavin.

EIGHT

"The backyard is clear," Gavin said after Brianne told him Stella had alerted and she'd heard something earlier. "You should have let me bring you home."

She sent him a controlled glare and went about finding plates and drinks. "Stella and I handled it, Gavin. I think someone had been in the yard and then hopped the fence when I sent Stella out. But they're gone now."

Gavin ignored the feminine glare and took in her home.

Small but tidy, showing signs of wear and tear, the living room consisted of a dark couch and a dainty side chair across from a broken-in, manly recliner with a table that held several television remotes. Family photos lined the walls—Brianne and her parents traveling together, her playing softball, taking karate lessons and winning awards in track and basketball. He noticed a tiny dog bed near the window. Surely not Stella's. Tommy noticed, too, and immediately starting sniffing.

"I could have gone over the fence to search."

"I told you I checked the yard and I did," she reminded him while she slapped pizza slices onto floral plates. "I also checked my apartment. The door was locked, and nothing has been tampered with." Seeing the direction of his gaze and Tommy's nose, she added, "My mom has a lap dog. Serpico is also an excellent guard dog, all ten pounds of him. But he's with her at the shore."

Obviously, he'd gone and made her mad with his heroic

efforts. Her comments were terse and her movements precise. She might throw a whole pizza at him.

But what should he do now?

She'd told him she thought someone had been in her yard the minute she'd opened the front door. He'd ignored her request to wait, and headed out back with Tommy to the small fenced yard, seeing it through the muted yellow of the security lights. A big oak and some shrubs, potted plants along the covered patio, and a door and a small patio to what must be her downstairs apartment. A door that made him nervous. The door where Stella had alerted. Tommy had gone over the entire small backyard and found no one and nothing. Just as she said—the door was secure.

"And I told you I'd do the same, so I did," he reminded her, still concerned about that vulnerable entryway. "It doesn't matter which one of us cleared the yard. We're here together."

"There's a thought," she retorted. "Us *working* together. I wanted to talk to you about that."

"Oh, so you bribed me with pizza to get me alone so you can remind me how you're just as capable as I am?"

She handed him his portion and then looked sheepish. "Something like that."

Tommy and Stella both lifted their heads. *Pizza?*

Gavin grabbed a big slice oozing with cheese and pepperoni. "I can't help being protective, Brianne. My grandmother was strong, but I always worried about her. It's my nature."

"Do I look like your grandmother?"

"Uh, no. She was pretty but you two are nothing alike."

"Maybe you can tell me all about her when we aren't both so tired and hyped-up?"

"Maybe I can and maybe I will," he replied, his eyes holding hers. "And maybe you can explain why a woman who grew up in a good home with solid parents decided to become a K-9 officer."

"Does that bother you—women in law enforcement? Is that why you can't let go and trust me?"

"No, no," he said, wishing Granny Irene had taught him how to talk to women without making them angry. "I'm all for women who want careers in law enforcement. It's not that at all. I admire you. I've told you that."

"Then what is it, Gavin?" she asked, her pizza chilling on the plate. "I can't shake the feeling that you're uncomfortable around me."

"I told you, I've never worked this closely with a female. Do you get that? I'm fighting that age-old problem— I'm attracted to you. I can't let that come between us but that does change things," he admitted. "You're pretty and scary-smart and determined. But we have to toe that line."

"You're right." Then she lifted her hand toward the back of the house. "I'm sorry. We rarely get intruders around here."

"Exactly," he said. "You handled it and the intruder is long gone. Your security and Stella worked, and you did your job."

"Except I overreacted about you," she said, lowering her eyes.

Surprised, Gavin shook his head. "So…you feel it, too?"

She looked flustered for about two seconds and then the wall came back down. "I've never worked with a man like you, Gavin. You stand out from the rest and you've stood up to the rest. But you give off a lot of mixed signals and I can't read any of them."

"I could say the same about you."

"My only signal is to do my job. That's it for now. I'm still a rookie. I can't afford any mess-ups. Especially the tangled-up-in-emotions kind. Get it?"

Yeah, he got it all right. That and the fact that someone had been snooping around her house. "We're a pair—full of our own angst and insecurities."

"Hey, speak for yourself," she teased. Then she nodded. "I think everyone has those issues but we all manage to hide our turmoil behind a wall of pride and determination."

"So can we work together and be professional, in spite of...whatever this is between us?"

"Can't be anything between us. Let's keep reminding ourselves of that."

"I guess I can do that." But inside, Gavin knew he'd be fighting a lot of battles while they were on this case. Something about holding her this afternoon in that mock embrace they'd shared just for show had made him think about her way too much. Her perfume, sultry and exotic. Her skin, warm and smooth. Her dress, so pretty and so perfect. Or the way she sighed, maybe without knowing she'd done it.

Gavin did a mental shake. He glanced up at her, trying to put a blank expression over some of that turmoil she'd mentioned.

Brianne handed him a soda and then sat down on the couch centered across from where he sat in the old recliner that had to be her father's favorite spot. The dogs settled at their feet, hoping for crumbs.

At least they weren't alerting. The intruder had obviously run away. But would he be back?

"We're in this together, Gavin. If you want me to have your back, you have to trust me to do my job."

"You still think I don't trust you? I just told you the truth."

She chewed her veggies-and-cheese and nodded. "Yes, and all of these feelings between us might get in the way and cause resentment and distrust. If you get aggravated and wish I wasn't around, you'll mess up by trying to do both our jobs. You'll consider me a distraction, a deterrent. That isn't going to cut it. So don't use that excuse again, okay?"

He sat there weighing his options. "You can walk away. No hard feelings."

"Are you having second thoughts?"

"First and second thoughts. This is an odd operation and I'm surprised Noah agreed to it. But he wants our department to shine, and so do I. If we nab the Tick, we all win."

"Not to mention we'd have something good to celebrate—getting an evil bomber and a corrupt real estate millionaire behind bars."

"That is cause for celebration. But we still have to help search for Chief Jordan's killer, too."

"We can do both, together. I'm good to go, Gavin. But if you're having doubts, all the more reason to tell me now. I can't fight that kind of waffling."

"The only waffling I do is at Griffin's on weekends when the price is reduced on a stack of 'em, Bree."

"Okay then. We can add an intruder in my backyard to our growing list of strange incidents. I could dust for prints or have the neighborhood searched, but we both know how this works. He's gone. I don't have a description and I can't even prove anyone was here."

"I'll search near the fence and see if he left anything. Footprints or something dropped."

"I'd feel better if we both did that." She waited a beat, but he didn't try to dissuade her.

Progress.

"About Griffin's," she said, not missing a beat. "Do you think what happened there has anything to do with the Tick and this case?"

"I think it might," he said, glad to be off the personal

stuff. "Lou said he'd been approached about selling. I've got Danielle and her crew looking at Lou's video footage and the traffic cams since a couple of the real estate agents came into the café and handed Lou cards. Maybe we can ID one of them."

"Good idea." Brianne took another bite of pizza. "Maybe Lou will remember more. Violet might not know about the details of the threats they could have received. They'd want to protect her, though."

"Lou didn't want to tell us from what I could see."

"I'm glad he did, even if the brokers weren't that threatening. More reason for us to be aware."

"But that means if they're after Lou, he and the whole staff as well as customers could be in danger. We were there, and the shooter saw, but I don't know if they specifically targeted us. Either way, that ups the danger on our play at being undercover." Giving her a frustrated stare, he added, "Now we have someone possibly snooping where you live, Bree. I don't like this. Maybe I should stay here with you."

"That would be a no," she quickly replied. "I can protect myself, Gavin."

"What if someone recognizes you while we're checking out apartments?"

"We're just looking at apartments. It's a free country. We can attend open houses like anyone else."

"Not so free if we snoop in the wrong places—together."

"Not so scary if we truly trust each other to the bitter end and stay alert and cautious until we have them behind bars."

Gavin picked up his third slice of pizza while he marveled at her reckless bravery. "I want to trust you, Brianne. But I brought you in on this. That means I feel obligated to watch out for you…"

"We can't let that get in our way, remember?" she said, dropping her pizza back on the plate in her hand. "You can't see me as anyone other than your current partner."

"I've never had a partner before. It's all new to me. But I believe you're the best person for the job."

"You mean, you believe I can stay professional? I can do that. Can you?"

He wondered at the blankness of her face and the darkness of her eyes. Could she really do that? Or would she put up that shield to protect her own confused feelings? "I'm working on being professional, yes. But it's different. We're playing a very real game."

She hid her surprise behind a stunned glare. "A little late to admit that, don't you think?"

"I'm not admitting anything." He sure wouldn't admit that he enjoyed being with her. "Are you still in?"

"I'm in," she replied. "In way too deep, but I'm in."

They finished their pizza, played with the dogs a bit, talked about their next plan of action and discussed the stall out on finding Jordan's killer.

But an awkward lull hung in the air, a sure sign that sooner or later, one of them would slip up and cross that line.

Gavin didn't want to be the first one to cave. When his cell buzzed, he gladly answered it.

"It's Danielle," he told Brianne.

She nodded and took the leftover pizza over to the kitchen and started cleaning up.

"What's up, Danielle?" he asked, hoping for a break.

"Nothing good," the fast-talking techie replied. "We can't get a read on the license plate of the Denali, Gavin. The surveillance camera in that area around Griffin's seems to be on the blink."

"You're kidding me, right?"

"I wish. A malfunction."

"That just figures," he said, frustration making him gruff. "Thanks, Danielle. I know you tried."

"It happens," she replied. "Those things are not one hundred percent accurate all the time."

"I know." He thanked her and closed his phone. Then he told Brianne. "We got nothing to go on yet on the shooting. Probably a rental vehicle. I'm sure whoever did this knows to cover their tracks but I worry that they sent someone here tonight."

Brianne came around the kitchen counter. "Danielle's right. Half the time, the cameras don't work or read false. And we don't know for sure a person was in my yard." Then she shook her head. "Who am I kidding? I heard footsteps—someone was running away."

"Just stay alert and keep the security lights on full blast. Set your alarm. We'll have to focus on the other evidence and hope we hear better news."

"And we have a plan," she reminded him. "That should keep us busy."

"A good plan," he said as she walked with him to the front door. "Lock up."

"And set the alarm," she repeated, but he saw the concern in her face. "Want me to follow you home and order you around? They might have paid your place a visit, too."

"No. I'm good."

He wasn't good, though. More like worried, confused and wide-awake. So he checked every corner of the rectangular Hayes house and did another sweep of her apartment door. Gavin didn't want to leave her there alone, but she wouldn't like him staying. At least Stella would alert on any noises, and she did have a motion-detector light on the back porch and a good security alarm.

But he circled the block two times before he headed

home. The surrounding streets were deserted and quiet. Brianne was smart, and she knew what to do if anyone returned to her house. So why was he so concerned?

Later this week, they'd tour a few more residential buildings and hope to get a lead on the Tick. Was he crazy for pursuing this?

Or was he crazy for letting Brianne Hayes get under his skin so quickly?

"We got a call about a possible sighting of Snapper near a construction site," Noah told Gavin the next morning. "I want you and Brianne to go and check things out. See if the dog is really Snapper."

"Okay," Gavin said just as Brianne came into the chief's office. Snapper was Jordan Jameson's missing partner. The dog had gone missing when Jordan had and though sightings had been reported, no one was sure if the German shepherd was really Snapper. He was still out there. They all desperately wanted to find the K-9—in honor of Jordan and because the dog was part of their family, part of their team. There was always a chance that finding Snapper would lead to a clue about Jordan's killer's identity. But at this point, they didn't know if the killer had taken the dog and let him go or if Snapper had been on the streets the entire time.

"You wanted to see me, sir?" She glanced from Noah to Gavin, her eyes wide with questions.

"Someone spotted a stray German shepherd," Gavin said. "Might be Snapper."

"Since you two are working together, I want you to partner up on this, too," Noah said, nodding. "Take both dogs with you, just in case. You can let them sniff around. ."

"Where?" Gavin asked, hoping the site wasn't one he'd been investigating.

The chief named a place near Flushing. "Let's go," he said to Brianne. "No time to waste."

Brianne nodded and made sure Stella had on her protective vest. Gavin could see the adrenaline in her bright eyes and stern expression. The woman was seriously into her work.

But then so was he. This tip could lead to nothing, but it might be another chance to help in solving Jordan's murder. If this dog turned out to be Snapper, it might lead them to evidence, somehow, some way. A long shot, but clues or not, the whole unit wanted Snapper back, safe and sound. Tommy and Stella were trained in bomb detection, but they could help out here, too. Tommy would recognize Snapper's scent and Stella would alert to another dog.

Work would keep his mind off Brianne and how she made him feel. Even if she stayed right by his side, Gavin knew one thing—they were both pros. He'd just have to tamp down these crazy currents of awareness he felt each time he got near the woman.

"Let's go together," she suggested. "I'll drive."

He didn't argue with her. She took off out the back door and headed to her vehicle.

"I'll check the area," he said, pulling out his phone. "I'm pretty sure I haven't done any searching or surveillance in this particular location but I do know some buildings in that part of the city are being gutted and renovated. Gentrification again."

"Let's hope not by our man," she replied as she gunned it through traffic like an expert race car driver.

Soon they were at the location. Nothing special but definitely not livable yet.

"An older building that's being renovated," Brianne said, her eyes wide. "Interesting."

"This one is not on my list," Gavin replied. "But that

doesn't mean an accident didn't happen months or years ago. I think this broker acts quickly and gets new construction going fast, probably cutting corners and breaking all kinds of union rules regarding safety. But I can't prove that on this one."

Brianne whirled into an open parking spot, the official vehicle giving them leverage if anyone complained. But the street around this area looked deserted, the building covered in scaffolding and construction dust.

This one stood at least twenty stories high. It had creamy old stone and black wrought-iron trim on the small balconies, rows of ornate windows and a quaintness that couldn't be denied.

"Let's check around the building first," Gavin suggested. "Looks like it covers half the block, at least."

They managed to find their way into an alley behind the main building. Tommy and Stella sniffed and glanced around but both appeared bored with the whole thing.

"I wonder if they *can* pick up Snapper's scent, like the chief said," Brianne whispered low.

"Maybe. But this could be a wild goose chase."

"Let's see."

They found an empty lot full of construction materials. Heavy plastic flapped in the moaning wind that flowed throughout the open, deserted building. But nobody seemed to be working here today.

"Odd, don't you think?" Gavin said, his words echoing out over the gutted building.

"Maybe they took a break or had a shutdown."

They kept moving. Brianne called out, "Snapper. Come."

Nothing happened except the haphazard rustling of plastic hitting against bricks, the sound of a few birds chirping in nearby trees and the constant noise of traffic out on the main thoroughfare.

They'd gone inside to check the gutted lobby area when they heard a yelp and then a bark. A scrawny, skinny dog came toward them at a slow bounce. When Tommy and Stella saw the other dog, they alerted and growled low.

Gavin gave Tommy the quiet sign. Stella calmed down after Brianne did the same.

Handing her leash off to Gavin, Brianne pulled out a treat and slowly made her way to the dog. "Here you go, boy. That's right. I won't hurt you."

She inspected the dog, careful to let him smell her knuckles and get to know her scent. Gavin watched, thinking the dog sure looked like Snapper but even from the distance of a few yards, he knew the truth. This dog wasn't a purebred German shepherd. Just a mutt out on the loose. They'd have to take him with them or call the pound to pick him up.

Brianne must have realized the same thing. She turned back to Gavin and shook her head. "It's not Snapper."

Disappointed, they told their K-9 partners to stay while they corralled the frightened, hungry animal, bribing him with treats until they had him inside the kennel in the SUV.

Leaving a vehicle window down, they turned to call their partners. "We'll put them in the backseat," Gavin said. He'd ask one of the trainers to evaluate the stray. The skinny mutt seemed calm and friendly, and maybe he could be trained as a service dog.

Gavin hated to tell the chief they hadn't found Snapper. Frustration heated him right along with the hot July sunshine.

They were headed back to the vehicle when Gavin heard a scraping noise, followed by several thuds and thumps above them. The dog waiting in the SUV went wild, barking and snarling, his head held up toward the roof.

Gavin glanced up and saw a steel beam barreling over the edge of an open high-up balcony—a beam coming down right toward them.

NINE

Gavin grabbed Brianne and shouted, "Go!" to the dogs.

Brianne looked up, her eyes going wide as the huge beam came tumbling toward them like a torpedo.

The dogs ran toward the SUV and turned to wait.

The stray barked from inside the open vehicle. His growl echoed out after the beam landed on the hard concrete with a deafening hit, cracking the pavement into chunks.

"Bree, are you okay?"

Brianne blinked and looked up at the man holding her, inhaling air full of dust and debris. Nodding, she said, "And you've saved me yet again."

Gavin moved away and then sat up at the same time she did. They'd landed in the grass near the alleyway. She already had enough bruises from being around this man.

"I see your wit and sarcasm are still intact," he said, getting up, craning his neck to squint up at the roof. "But your new pal there in the vehicle saved us. Apparently, that dog knows whoever was on that roof."

"Did you see someone?" She hopped up before he could offer her his hand. "We need to search this whole place."

"I didn't see anything but the beam coming down." Gavin stared up toward the balcony. "But by the way the stray barked, I'm thinking that beam didn't just fall off the roof by itself. Someone had to have pushed it."

"Only one way to find out," Brianne said, courage she

didn't feel coloring her words. "We call for backup and go up there in the meantime."

They took Stella and Tommy and hurried into the building to the service elevator. "It's working," Gavin said as he punched buttons.

The rickety contraption made a groaning climb and caused Brianne to consider the stairs. But they didn't have time for that. Soon they were crawling at a snail's pace toward the roof.

Brianne followed him out onto the scorching hot rooftop, the view grabbing her. She could just make out the East River off to the west. She scanned the area, noticing building materials and a stack of beams like the one that had fallen.

"Gavin," she said, indicating something she'd spotted in a corner.

He followed her gaze. "Let's go."

They hurried the dogs over to the corner. Tommy immediately alerted, his doleful gaze on Gavin.

"He's picked up something," Gavin whispered.

"I know what it is," Brianne said, already snapping photos with her cell. "A plaid baseball cap."

Stella caught the wind and gave Brianne her own signal that she recognized this item, too.

Gavin did a sweep of the entire roof. "No one. No place to hide and we came up the only working elevator."

He leaned over and checked below. "Whoever did this sure got away fast."

"And left his hat behind," Brianne said, grabbing a pen out of her pocket and lifting the hat with it. "We can bag this when we get back to our vehicle."

"This was no accident, Bree," he said, a frown coloring his sweat-drenched skin. "And it wasn't a coincidence that we were sent here."

"Nope. The Fourth of July bomber could have been here."

"Or someone wearing a plaid hat and trying to mess with us was here. Someone who doesn't want us to find Jordan's killer." Gavin turned and went to another door leading into the building. "This is locked tight, but they could have had a key and they might have taken the stairs."

"We'll have to take the elevator again and check the stairs from the ground up."

They made it down without any more mishaps. After bagging the hat and placing it on the floor behind the passenger seat, Brianne checked on the dog in the SUV, gave him some nibbles and made sure he had water and that the windows were open halfway.

Then they headed to the first set of stairs, only to find the door locked.

Hitting her hand on the steel door, she said, "He planned this so he could take the stairs and get away while we rode that old elevator."

Gavin looked around. "We can take the elevator again and search floor by floor until backup arrives."

"Good idea, but what about the dog in the SUV? Scrawny."

"Bring him just in case they're still lurking," Gavin said, noting the nickname. "Scrawny is now an honorary member of the K-9 Unit, plus he might find the intruder. We'll deputize him."

Brianne ran to the SUV and got the dog out. When she heard sirens echoing out over the street, she breathed a sigh of relief. With a little effort, she had Scrawny leashed and ready to go, giving him treats to entice him.

They started the long, rigorous climb on the rickety iron-gated elevator. On each floor, they moved through the open units, letting the dogs lead the way.

Gavin talked into the radio to the patrol officers who'd arrived, telling them to search down below.

An hour later, nothing. The dogs had sniffed the air and the ground. Scrawny seemed to get the importance, the poor boy lifting his head like a pro. They did find a water dish and bowl on the fourth floor.

At least the dog had been taken care of while the suspect waited for them to show up. Nothing else there, though.

Bree took an evidence bag from one of the other officers and wrapped the dog bowls inside it. "Maybe we'll get a hit on a print."

Gavin rubbed a hand down his face. "I doubt it."

Brianne felt his frustration. "We were set up."

"Yep," Gavin said. "Now it's personal. He knows about Jordy's death—or someone involved in this knows and called in a fake sighting of Snapper. Noah picked us randomly to check it out, but whoever was waiting probably recognized us."

"Do you think the two are connected? The bomber and Jordan's death? Did someone set this up because we're looking into real estate? Or does someone want to distract our unit from finding out the truth about Jordan's murder?"

"Good question. I don't know. But I do believe our suspect is keeping up with the news updates and he—or whoever they sent to do this today—knew that Snapper is still missing. So they used Scrawny to lure someone from our department here."

"So what now?" Brianne asked. Scrawny seemed to fit right in. The two K-9s sniffed him with a keen interest and he returned the gesture. He might make a good service dog yet. Or maybe a K-9.

"We didn't find any scent of a bomb, so that's that. He's long gone and the only evidence we have is that cap."

Walking in a pacing circle, she turned back to Gavin. "Well, the dogs were smart enough to pick up on that hat. Maybe, just maybe, the lab can, too." Then she pointed to Scrawny. "Stella and Tommy picked up his scent. He might have some evidence in his fur."

Gavin moved toward the SUV. "We need to get Scrawny to the vet. I'll dust the door to the stairs for prints, but I'm guessing I won't find much. Then we'll turn over the evidence to the lab."

Brianne wiped at her wet brow. "Always exciting, working with you, Sutherland."

"Same here, Hayes."

"I need a hamburger," she decided. "Too many near-death experiences have made me see the light."

"And what do you see in that light?" he asked after they had the animals watered and settled in the back of the SUV.

"Besides my maker?" She gave him a soft smile. "That life is too short not to really live. And living means eating a burger when under stress."

"Amen to that. Hamburgers it is. But after we get all of this squared away."

Brianne wondered if they'd ever get any of this squared away. She glanced at Scrawny. "Gavin, I can't stop thinking about the setup."

"What about it?"

"Someone wanted us to think we'd find Snapper at this location, right?"

"I believe we've established that, yes. Noah told me about the dog first thing this morning."

"But *who* called Noah? No one could guess he'd send us. But whoever it was wanted us dead. Because we're investigating Jordan's murder? Because we're investigating the Fourth of July bomb? Was it the same guy who shot at us at Griffin's? What is going on?"

Gavin met her gaze head-on. "All very good questions we don't have the answers to. But we'll have to find them—soon."

* * *

"An anonymous tip," Noah said an hour later after the whole team had gathered for their daily reports on Jordan's murder. He'd brought his assistant, Sophie Walters, in to verify that. "I find it hard to believe your bomber or anyone connected to my brother's death left that dog there."

"Do you think that beam falling was coincidence then, sir?" Brianne asked.

Carter Jameson tapped his fingers on the table. "Noah, you have to see this isn't a coincidence. What would cause a beam to fall like that? It's not that windy out today. And no one was around working. Sounds like a setup to me."

Gavin shot Carter a thankful glance. Brianne's gazed moved from Carter to his brother Noah. The chief remained quiet.

Gavin spoke up. "I don't think this incident has anything to do with Jordan's death but I do believe it has everything to do with the Fourth of July bomber. He knows Brianne and I saw him at the park that day. Brianne and Stella gave chase but lost him in the crowd. He's probably been keeping up with our entire department and Jordan's case. The only way he'd know we'd be the two to show up is if he's been following us. Today he had an opportunity to do something. It started with the shooting at Griffin's—whether the bullets were aimed at us or to harass Lou, we don't know—and Brianne had a breach in her backyard last night."

"Honestly, you believe that?" Luke Hathaway asked.

Luke, of all people, should know anything was possible. He'd saved Jordan's administrative assistant, Sophie Walters, from the man who tried to kill her after she witnessed him leave a phony suicide note from Jordan in with some of Jordan's paperwork. Claude Jenks wouldn't reveal who'd hired him, and had been struck by a car and killed while running from police.

Luke and Sophie were engaged now. When she'd reported on the anonymous call about Snapper earlier, she'd smiled at Luke in passing. Their love shone so brightly that Gavin had wanted to look away. Instead, he'd looked at Brianne.

"I do believe that, Luke," he said. "We got shot at the other day at Griffin's. And the morning after the park bombing at that."

"Yeah, but we all agree Lou might have been the target. We're keeping a close eye on his place," Noah said, his arms crossed in a firm stance.

"We think someone is after us," Gavin replied without going into detail about his undercover plan.

Noah sent him a hard stare. "We can't trace the call. They didn't stay on the line long enough."

"I figured as much," Gavin said. "I think it was a setup. We checked the roof and there is no way a beam could have just toppled over. Someone had to have placed it near the edge and then tossed it down."

Brianne stood up. "We found a cap that looks like the same one the bomber wore—red, white and blue plaid. The lab is testing it along with some fibers found on the dog. Gavin dusted for prints around the door to the first-floor stairs and we have two dog dishes that could hold some DNA or prints. We think the Fourth of July bomber was at that building today because he's been tracking us since we spotted him in the park."

Gavin stood with her. "I agree, and I stand by everything Brianne and I have reported."

Noah dismissed the others and then stood with them. "Do I need to take you off this real estate bombing case?"

"No, sir," they both said at once.

"We're making progress," Gavin said. "A week or so more."

"Okay," Noah said. "I have to admit today's incident does sound fishy but we need solid proof that any of this is connected. We'll see what the lab says, all right?"

They left defeated. Gavin wanted to hit a wall. "What do I have to do to prove to him that I'm not crazy?

"We'll make him a believer," Brianne replied, steel behind that declaration. "The bomber doesn't know we went undercover. He might only know us as two K-9 officers who got a good look at him."

Gavin wished he hadn't gotten her involved. Now Noah had her on his radar, too.

Brianne kept walking, but he stopped her when they neared the back entrance to the building. "Hey, you don't have to keep at this."

Brianne turned to give him a frown. "I'm not quitting, Gavin. I know someone is after us so we have to stay one step ahead of them. Do you honestly think I'd just walk away after you've come to my rescue twice now?"

Gavin's heart did a funny little leap. Joy, maybe?

"No one's ever said anything like that to me before."

Brianne's frown softened. "Your granny had *your* back."

"She did, but she never needed rescuing."

And the frown came back. "But I do, right? I need rescuing, Gavin?"

"No, Bree, I do," he said. Then he turned and headed out the door before he did something stupid like tug her close and hold her tight.

TEN

Brianne couldn't get Gavin's words out of her head.

Did he need rescuing?

The man seemed so confident and sure at times, then demonstrated the same insecurities and frustrations that hit her almost every day.

After letting Stella sniff the backyard and clear the upstairs, she went down to her apartment and made sure everything was as she'd left it. Stella sniffed here and there but didn't indicate anything out of the ordinary.

"I don't know, Miss Stella," she said, glad she had someone to vent to. "How's it coming with Tommy? I mean, I know he's not as tall as you but that dog has a heart of gold and he has that striking brown mask-like pattern on his face with matching brown spots. And those floppy ears—so adorable. He's a true hero. You guys make a cute couple."

Stella stared up at her with somber golden-brown eyes, then plopped on her big dog bed and put her nose down on her paws.

"Now you look as confused as me," Brianne noted. "Males can do that. Both the human and the dog kind. I'm going to take a shower and then we'll decide about dinner. Because Gavin never did take me to get a hamburger."

A few minutes later, Brianne stared at the empty refrigerator in her apartment and thought about going upstairs to raid her mom's freezer. But while her parents often invited her up for meals, Brianne insisted on paying for her own groceries and her part of the utilities. Her father had recently retired after working for the city for twenty-five years.

She hadn't mentioned this to Gavin, but hearing her dad's stories when he'd worked in the transportation department had shaped her career choice. His proud talk about the brave men and women of the New York Police Department had been the main reason she'd decided to become a cop. That and her love for animals had sealed her decision to become a K-9 officer.

Now she had finally begun living her dream job, frustrations aside. She'd made it to the top of her class and the only mar had been the chief's horrible death. She didn't mind holding off on the official graduation ceremony but... she wished their class hadn't been hit with such a tragedy right out of the gate.

And somehow she'd also stumbled into an unusual assignment with an interesting, slightly uptight partner.

Stumbled, or had a push from the Big Man upstairs?

Lord, if You want me here, could You steer me through? she prayed.

"I didn't ask for a partner."

Stella lifted her head.

"I'm not talking about you, Miss Stella," Brianne corrected. "You are the best partner in the history of partners."

Stella did a little woof and then got up to stare at her food bowl. Brianne took the hint and fed her loyal friend.

When her phone rang, Brianne hurried to grab it. Probably her parents calling in with a report on how much fun they were having. They often stayed for weeks during the summer in her aunt and uncle's beach house. Brianne usually visited them a couple of times on weekends, but another visit would have to wait for now.

Not bothering to check the caller ID, she said, "Hayes."

"Uh…it's Gavin. I have a bag of burgers and… I'm parked in front of your house. Are you hungry?"

"Starving," she said. "Come in the door to my apartment. Just go around to the gate and come through the yard."

"I'm on my way."

"Gutsy of him," she said to Stella. "Driving across town and showing up unannounced."

When she heard a knock at the door opening to the tiny porch that served as her private sunning area, she looked through the blinds to make sure it was Gavin.

He shook the white bag at her.

Brianne opened the door and smiled. "You went to the Shake Shack?"

"Yes. Is that okay?"

She yanked him inside and shut the door, Tommy on his heels. "Only if you got me the cheeseburger with all the trimmings."

"I did."

Stella perked up and stood to greet her friend Tommy. The smaller dog yelped at her, his curly brown-and-cream spotted fur almost bristling with delight. Stella played it cool but gave him a doggie smile.

Brianne wished humans could figure each other out so quickly.

Gavin glanced around and she cringed at her messy home. "I'm not good at domestic stuff."

He took in the small kitchen where a few dishes sat on the draining board, and the living area cluttered with books, magazines and training manuals, before giving Brianne a thumps-up. He smiled at Stella who stood with Tommy, both curious about what came next, then pointed to the superhero-embossed throw on the bright blue love-seat. "That's interesting."

"It makes me feel safe," she said with a shrug, glad she'd at least lit a spicy-smelling candle. "Since I seem to need saving a lot."

"You don't need a superhero, Bree," he said, his gaze moving over her.

"But I do need a burger."

Soon, they were sitting at the tiny kitchen table inhaling burgers and fries, the dogs hovering nearby after they'd both been fed their rations for the day.

"You didn't have to do this, Gavin," she said. "Driving all the way over here and stopping to get food, too."

"I wanted to apologize for how we left things this afternoon."

She chewed on a fry. "You mean, the fact that we didn't get lunch and now I'm woofing down this food too fast because I'm starving?"

"Yeah, that and how I implied certain things."

"Oh, the part about me rescuing you?"

"That, yes. Just one of my moods."

"*I* never get moody."

He took her seriously. "You don't seem to. In fact, you seem to have life figured out."

"Ha. I don't have anything figured out." She wiped her fingers on a napkin. "But Gavin, you *do* need rescuing—from yourself."

"Excuse me?"

"You want what you want and there is nothing wrong with that. But you can't seem to see that you're good and you're kind and you work hard. Surely your grandmother taught you all those things, so you must see them in yourself."

He frowned and put down his burger. "My grandmother was a good, hardworking woman who sacrificed a lot for me."

She could tell he wanted to say more but wasn't ready to spill his guts to Brianne.

"She raised you, right?"

He nodded, his eyes dark with emotion. "Yes, but…"

"But what, Gavin? I need to understand why you seem to have a big chip on your shoulder."

He dropped his napkin and stared over at her. "Why do you need to pry? You had a family, Bree. Two parents, married and solid. A good house to live in. Stability. You didn't have to second-guess everything you did or said."

"And because of that, I'm somehow okay?" She laughed. "I've had to fight and scrape for all of it, Gavin. I had to beg my parents to let me try out for the Police Academy. My dad had seen the worst of this city and he hated the idea of me being out there on the streets. But I wanted it—because he'd also worked those streets in the transportation department. He knew them in and out, and I loved hearing his stories. But he didn't want me to know or see that kind of life."

"Bree—"

"No, let me finish. My mom worked as a school secretary and dealt with the worst of teenagers and my dad saw a lot of horrible things. They tried to protect me, but I felt stifled at times. So I haven't had it all that great but I had a pretty good life with parents who loved me and now, even with their concerns, they support me."

Gavin got up and turned to stare down at her. "Granny Irene loved me, too. But…she never got over how my mother just up and left me at her doorstep, an obligation to her."

Brianne's stomach clenched. "I didn't know that."

"I don't talk about it much."

"Well, your grandmother had to have loved you and

apparently she took good care of you. Did she live long enough to see you join the force?"

He nodded. Then he shrugged. "But I never felt as if I measured up to her dreams—the dreams she had for my mother."

"Maybe you're wrong," Brianne said. "Maybe she loved by actions, not words. And that counts for something."

He stared down at her and shook his head. "You amaze me. You're full of bluster and sarcasm but underneath, you have a big heart."

"I could say the same for you. Now sit back down and finish your burger. We're still a team, okay?"

"Okay."

He'd just reached for his burger when his burner phone rang.

"It's Justin Sanelli," he told Brianne after glancing at the caller ID. "I think things are about to get rolling."

Brianne stood beside him and nudged him to answer. "I'm ready. I've got your back, Gavin."

Gavin gave her an appreciative glance and took the call. He turned to Brianne after he'd disconnected. "He wants to show us another property. This one in a building in Tribeca."

Brianne cleared away the remains of their meal. "That's gonna be pricey."

"Yes, this is an open house, so others will be around."

"Do you think the Tick will show up?"

"If he does, he'll be in disguise just like us."

"What if he remembers Tommy?"

"There are a lot of springer spaniels in New York."

She smiled at Tommy. "I'll find him another interesting dog collar."

Tommy's eyes widened in protest. Gavin thought the dog always stayed one step ahead of them.

Brianne motioned to the love seat and she took the cushioned rocking chair across from it. "Why a new building?"

"I'm wondering about that," he admitted after he settled onto the comfortable little sofa. "I can't see anyone bombing such expensive property."

"Maybe Justin wants to impress us with his clients. We might see some celebrities or high-ranking New Yorkers."

"We need to be careful, though."

"Okay, so we go to the open house, act impressed and make our way around while stressing we want in on any property that needs to be torn down. And we watch for the Tick."

"I think that's a good plan. The Tick could be scouting us out, too."

She pushed at her hair, which was down tonight. A treat for Gavin—he wanted to run his hands through all those reddish-brown waves. Her hair had to be so soft.

"And still no word on whether the Tick is William Caston—the man I thought looked like him in his mug shot?"

"Nope. We can't find him to bring him in, which makes me think he has to be the Tick. That man knows how to go to ground."

"Well, if he's working for Sanelli, he might be attending the open house and could soon be high in the sky with us," she quipped."

When she got up to put her glass in the sink, Gavin gently held her wrist. "Bree, we have to be careful."

She studied his hand on her and nodded. "I will be careful, Gavin. You have to trust me."

He stood and held her gaze. "I keep telling you, I do trust you and appreciate you. But that doesn't mean I don't worry."

"We aren't in the business of worrying," she retorted. "We never have time for that. And I'd rather not think about it and just do the job."

"And I'd rather be prepared and think things through." He shrugged. "My grandmother always had her ducks in a row. When my mother left and never looked back, it shattered Granny Irene's methodical, controlled little world. She lost her husband early on, so she had reason to worry and fret but she held it together. Too much at times, I think. I guess I inherited some of that resolve and pride."

"And...you never got closure with your mother, right?"

"That is another whole conversation," he said, wishing he could let go of the shadow that seemed to follow him around. "Let's save that for another time."

Her expression softened and she pulled away. "Okay, back to the case then. I'm the rookie, so you do the heavy strategizing and I'll do what I need to do when it's time to make a move, all right?"

"As long as we're on the same page."

"I'm there, Gavin. I just want you to see that I'm there. I'm not going to abandon you or let you down."

He motioned to Tommy and headed for the door, uncomfortable with her pointed promise. "I see more than you think," he said. "I'm gonna go home and do some research on this apartment building so I'm prepared."

"And I'll do the same," she said, her tone firm. "Plus, I have to figure out what to wear."

"It's Tribeca," he reminded her. "Understated and hip."

She made a face at his effort to talk uppity. "I think I can handle that."

"You'd look good in a flour sack."

"Nope. Not gonna happen."

He nodded at her and Tommy barked at Stella. "I'll see you tomorrow."

"Thanks for the burgers." Brianne shut the door with a thud.

"Search," Gavin whispered to Tommy. She might think she had it all together but...he had the right to watch her back.

"What she doesn't know won't hurt her, right?"

Tommy seemed to bob his head, but Gavin knew the dog was doing a ground-to-air search.

They covered the whole backyard but Tommy didn't alert. The only sound came from a rickety swing under a mushrooming oak tree. The dog turned to stare up at Gavin. *What next?*

"Good job, Tommy," Gavin said, keeping his words low. For now, Brianne was safe.

ELEVEN

At the briefing on Jordan's murder case the next morning, Noah told the team they still had nothing much to go on. "We've had sightings on dogs we thought might be Snapper, but we haven't found him yet. We thought we had a solid lead yesterday but while Gavin and Brianne found a dog similar to Snapper, he turned out to be a mix—part German shepherd and part hound, we think."

K-9 Officer Lani Branson spoke up. "His nickname is Scrawny, but we'll get him healthy and change that," she said with a smile. "I'm working with him to see if he has K-9 or service dog capabilities. I'm thinking the latter since he's calm and has a big heart. He's been checked out and given his shots and he's had a couple of decent meals. Ynez says he's malnourished but she's taking care of that."

Everyone smiled. Ynez Dubois, one of the best veterinarians in the city, took care of all of the K-9s and any strays they brought in, too.

"Well, at least we have a new prospect," Noah said, his tone full of disappointment about the dog not turning out to be Snapper. "We'll make sure the stray finds a good home, whether inside the department or in the service dog capacity."

"We have to find Snapper. For Jordan. And we have to find Jordy's killer," Zach reminded them, his blue eyes flashing with anger over his brother's death. "Snapper is out there somewhere. We can't stop looking."

Gavin gave him a sympathetic glance. Jordan's brothers

were still grieving. It would take a long time to deal with his death, but they needed solid answers and some closure. At least Zach had Violet to help him through. Those two had been neighbors growing up, but a threat on Violet's life that involved a drug dealer and a reluctant coworker smuggling shipments into the airport had brought them together as a couple.

Once they were dismissed and heading out for the day, Gavin called out. "Brianne?"

Brianne turned at the door to the parking lot. "Hey."

Waiting until they were alone, he nodded to her. "So let's meet at the Gable again. The building we're going to is on the corner of Hudson and Reade in Tribeca. I'll pick you up at the safe house so we can pull up in the car together. There's valet parking."

"Okay. What time?"

"It starts at six. So around that time. We don't want to look too anxious and be the first to arrive."

"Oh, no, of course not."

"Just so you know, I can't locate my CI, Beanpole. He must be on the move. He has different corners where he hangs out but no one's seen him for a while."

"So no verification on Plaid Cap being the man he heard discussing this with another man."

"No, not yet. But I'm thinking the other man had to be Justin Sanelli."

"And we still don't have the DNA results, if any, from the fibers and other evidence we sent to the lab."

They parted, and Gavin saw Brianne stop to talk to Lani and their friend Faith, a seasoned K-9 officer who'd helped train Brianne. The women's expressions changed from happy to curious to surprised to intrigued. He had to wonder what *that* conversation was all about.

* * *

"What gives, Bree?" Faith asked, her dark eyebrows slashed up, her short hair curling around her jawline.

"What are you talking about?" Brianne asked, glancing from Lani to Faith. She'd neglected her friends lately and now they wanted answers.

"You don't have time for a night out and I heard Gavin making a date with you."

"It's not like that," she tried to explain as they left the building and headed to their vehicles.

"Then what is it like?" Lani asked, tossing her blond ponytail. "You two seem awfully chummy lately."

Brianne glanced around. How to handle this?

"She's hedging," Faith said. "What are you not telling us?"

"We're still working this case," she said on a low whisper. "The Fourth of July bombing case I mentioned before. For our protection, we're trying to keep details under wraps."

"Oh, for your protection," Lani teased. Then she turned serious. "We get it. You don't need to explain since we're all concerned about this so-called bomber."

"Can we talk later?" Brianne said. "I have to do some training with Stella this morning."

"I'm headed that way myself," Lani said. "I want to take a look at Scrawny."

"I have to hit the street," Faith replied. "Lunch soon?"

"The Pizza Palace? Friday?" Lani said, giving Brianne a questioning stare.

"I can do that," Brianne replied, hoping she'd be able to keep that promise.

She hurried toward the training center with Lani, glad her friend didn't push for more information. She wanted to work off some steam with Stella this morning since the

Labrador wouldn't be with them tonight. She also wanted to check on Scrawny.

"Maybe we should have nicknamed our new dog Brawny since he'd obviously been dumped on the streets and left for dead," she said to Lani. "He's a scrapper, no doubt. A survivor."

"He'll be fine once we get him fattened up with good food and get him into training." Her friend gave her a worried glance. "Hey, are you okay, Bree?"

"Just thinking about that poor dog. He went with us up to the roof, you know. He bonded with us right away. If he hadn't made such a fuss, we might not have seen that beam. He probably saved our lives."

Lani gave her an empathetic smile. "You survived and so did the dog—an animal probably abused at the hands of this person. Your kindness to Scrawny made him immediately bond with you and the K-9s. A lesson for all of us."

"Jordan was brawny and tough," Brianne said, the image of the chief being forced to write that horrible suicide note moving through her head. "Why didn't he survive? Why would someone kill him and make it look like a suicide?"

Lani shook her head. "I don't have the answer to that, but each time we get a lead, it's another opportunity to find out the truth. We might find something on the dog you brought in or on the hat and those food dishes. It's not over yet."

"You're right. We're still waiting on the lab for DNA from the bomb fragments we found after the Fourth of July... We've got a name, but we can't find the man. Maybe something will develop with that, too."

"Is that why you're not quite yourself?" her friend asked while they headed down the hall to the outside training facility. "Are you still shaken from the bomb scare?"

"Maybe," Brianne admitted. "Made me stop and think."

"About mortality and men?"

"About mortality and one man," she admitted.

"I knew it," Lani said. "You and Gavin have a certain chemistry."

"I *don't* know it yet," she retorted. "Or rather, I'm trying to ignore that chemistry. That's not easy and I'm not ready to talk about it."

Lani nodded. "Tell me when you're ready, because it's becoming more and more obvious to all of us."

Brianne wanted to say more, but then she wasn't ready to tell her friends much about her feelings for Gavin. She wanted to see where they went with this case and then… later they'd decide about that chemistry Lani seemed to think they had.

Brianne's gut burned for answers on the bomber and on finding the person responsible for the chief's murder. It didn't matter how many times they went over what little evidence they had, getting a fresh lead would really help all of them right now. Yesterday, finding that dog had given her hope. But then almost getting crushed by a beam had dashed those hopes.

"Maybe today will be the day, Lani," she said. "Maybe we'll get news that can help all of us to understand why Jordan had to die."

Lani nodded. "I'll pray for that end, Bree."

Brianne followed her friend out onto the training arena. This spot always brought her calm and peace. She loved working with the handlers and watching the dogs grow and become confident in what they were trained to do. After one of the trainers brought out Scrawny, Brianne gave him a rub and grinned at the eager dog.

"Go on, boy. You're already a hero in my eyes."

Brianne took over with Stella while Lani patiently learned what kind of stuff Scrawny was made of.

Brianne and Stella worked the obstacle courses and went through their paces on hide-and-seek so Stella would continue to improve on sniffing out incendiary devices. One of the lead trainers who'd worked with Stella came over to talk about how far she had come.

"You *are* a smart girl," Brianne told her furry partner a couple of hours later. "You found the goods so now we have playtime."

Stella's ears perked up. She'd worked hard after being a good, attentive mother to her puppies. Now they were all being fostered by various members of the K-9 team to learn socialization before they started intense training. When Brianne played a game of tug-of-war with her, Stella growled and snarled in a playful way, determined to hang onto the prize. Then they played fetch for a while. Stella loved running after a soft plastic ball but Brianne didn't allow her to keep it or chew on it. If Stella swallowed a chunk of the ball's shell, she could die from a stomach obstruction.

"Let's go get cleaned up," Brianne said. "And we'll get a treat."

Stella knew what that word meant.

At the end of the shift, Brianne left Stella clean and fed inside the kennel room. "I'll be back to get you later tonight, I promise."

Brianne had to go and get gussied up for the big open house in Tribeca.

Would she come face-to-face with a bomber?

Gavin stood in the hotel suite doorway, admiring Brianne's outfit. She grinned at him, looking like she was waiting for a friend. She'd dressed in a beige lightweight

T-shirt with a black scarf looped over a flowing paisley skirt with black strappy sandals. Her hair was dark again but down, cascading around her face in a casual toss, her bangs hooding her eyes. Dangling gold earrings swung against her neck. And she carried another expensive-looking purse with some designer's initials on it.

"Hello, beautiful."

Shaking her head, she asked, "Is that part of the act?"

"No, you *are* beautiful. But, yes, I know the rules."

"Tonight, we pretend there are no rules."

"You look different," he said to push past that statement. "I mean, you really are in disguise."

"That's what layers of mascara and eyeliner can do for a person," she quipped.

"Maybe I should ditch the mustache and try that," he retorted.

That made her laugh. "I kinda think the mustache is a better look on you."

She had her look down—expensive but bohemian, understated but fashionably cool. While he liked her red hair better, he had to admit the dark brown looked real good.

Sure beat their official uniforms. He followed her to their waiting car. Tommy did a tailspin and stared out the window, his happy face greeting her.

"I feel the same way," Gavin whispered before she slid into the car.

"You clean up nicely, too," Brianne said once they were buckled in.

"I dress this way when I'm off duty."

She laughed again, the sound dancing around him like tiny bells. "Sure you do."

He'd worn jeans and a sport coat that would have cost a week's salary, except he'd found it at a thrift store with the tags still on it. His dark shades helped to hide his eyes. "It's showtime."

He weaved in and out of side streets jutting off from Broadway to avoid traffic.

"The Bec-Off-Broadway," Brianne said as they came to a stop about thirty minutes later in front of the chrome-and-glass lobby. "A brand new building. So this is what happens when people get bombed out of their homes."

"Collateral damage to the person responsible. They don't care about people being forced out of their homes, or buildings having to come down because of corruption."

"Well, we do," she reminded him. "I hope we find something to help us."

"Yeah, I hope so, too."

He got out and came around to open her door, surprised that he let her. But when she stepped out, he understood she was playing her part. She held the seat up so Tommy could jump out of the car. Then she placed a black leather dog collar around the K-9's neck and winked at Gavin.

"I like having matching accessories," she said with a feminine grin, her finger pointing to the wide leather band on her left arm.

Gavin laughed and nodded. "That's so you, darling."

To prying eyes, they looked like a happy, flirting couple.

But Gavin could see the shimmer of intensity in her dark eyes, could feel the heat of excitement running through her veins. Brianne lived for this stuff while he only wanted to do the job and get back to being a K-9 cop.

Tommy felt it, too. He might be playing a pampered pooch but the K-9 also knew he had work to do. He danced and watched Gavin's face for his orders.

The valet took the key to the car. "Nice ride, dude."

"Thanks," Gavin said, giving him the alias of Linus

Reinhart. Then he handed the kid a big tip. "Take care of it for me, will you?"

The young man bobbed his head. "Don't you know it!"

Gavin held Brianne's arm as they made their way into the glimmering lobby of the building. An agency rep showed them the private elevator to the top floor of the ten-story building.

"Based on the history of this location before this place came up, I'd say the older building was cozy and could have been salvaged," Brianne whispered. "It's a shame that it had to be torn down."

Gavin nodded. "Yep. A fire destroyed the bottom three floors. They had to condemn the building."

"But no one found the truth."

He shook his head since the elevator had stopped. "Not yet." Then he leaned close, as if he were whispering sweet nothings into her ear. "But we're here to take care of that."

When the door opened, Brianne was staring into his eyes, her smile frozen on her face. Gavin held her gaze. "Be careful," he reminded her. "Please."

TWELVE

Brianne followed Gavin's lead. She kept her gaze on him for a brief moment and then turned to find several sets of curious but cool eyes on both of them.

Inhaling, she let go of Gavin's arm and held Tommy by his leash, steadying him as they entered the ritzy crowd. People dressed in glittering clothes, torn jeans with diamonds, bright blond long hair with short red dresses, short dark bobs and all black clothing, men in button-up shirts and polished loafers, some in suits with glee in their eyes. Some ignoring everything and everyone while they stared at the incredible view of historic townhouses and the Hudson River off in the distance.

She noticed a woman doing just that, a champagne glass in her hand, a diamond tennis bracelet sparkling against her porcelain skin. Her inky black hair fell in expensive layers down over her shoulders. Her cream-colored suit shouted Armani.

And when she turned, her eyes caught Brianne's. A cold smile and then the woman moved on.

Something about the other woman left Brianne cold, too. Too rich to be friendly.

Before she could say anything to Gavin, Justin Sanelli hurried toward them. "The Reinharts. So glad you came. Grab some champagne and I'll personally give you the tour. I think you'll like this place."

Brianne made a face. "But, Justin, this is all new and

shiny. We wanted to find a fixer-upper. You know, a building we can put our own stamp on."

"Of course," the agent said. He twisted the gold ring he wore on his left finger. "Just see what you think and then I'll explain how to make that dream come true." Then he laughed. "The previous building on the property was in a mess when we bought it. Crumbling and out of date and most of it destroyed by a tragic fire. We've built one of the most sought-after properties in Tribeca."

"I'm impressed," Brianne said with a smile, while she sent Gavin a knowing nod. Justin obviously loved making things happen in the real estate world.

He moved them through the crowd with ease, smiling and patting people on the back as he went. Brianne had worried about people wanting to pet Tommy but others had brought lap dogs in huge purses, while some held tiny dogs in their arms, so what was one more animal in the crowd?

Tommy marched along with her. Gavin warned her Tommy might not pick up a scent with so many perfumes and other scents merging in the spacious living and kitchen areas of the apartment. The dog, used to crowds, had been trained on how to react and not react, but this crowd was different.

Tommy, however, did his job in a subtle way, sniffing here and there, his head going up and then down. So far, he hadn't alerted on anyone in particular.

"Let's start with the master bedroom," Justin said as he moved up a short staircase. "It covers the entire top floor, closet space is huge and the bathroom is like a spa."

They passed the dark-haired woman on the stairs. Justin stopped, twisting his ring. "Liza, I'd like you to meet the Reinharts. They're interested in renovating property in Manhattan."

"You've come to the wrong place," the woman he'd

called Liza said, her voice cultured and crisp. "We just finished this building. We had to start from scratch but… don't you think the results were worth the effort?"

Brianna shot Gavin a quick glance and then held out her hand to the woman. "It's a beautiful place."

Justin moved to say something but was interrupted.

"Liza Collins," the woman said, her hand cold against Brianne's skin. "Justin mentioned you two just the other day."

"Did he now?" Gavin asked, looking bored. "We thought we'd stop by, but we're looking for something a bit different—Alice has a thing for authentic art deco and prewar designs."

"Maybe we can persuade you on this one," Liza said, her cold eyes assessing them.

"Liza owns the Rexx Agency," Justin explained.

Gavin nodded. "Ah. So you're the famous Mrs. Watson Collins."

"I am," she replied. "But I'm a widow now as most of New York knows."

Gavin lowered his head. "I'm sorry for your loss."

"So am I," the cold woman replied. "But yes, the Rexx Agency is still going strong in spite of everything. And Justin is my top broker," she said, almost cooing. "You're in good hands. Come and have more refreshments after your tour."

Brianne wanted to shudder but she held herself erect. So Liza was *that* Collins. The name had sounded familiar. A big scandal a few years back regarding corruption and embezzlement in the real estate world.

Tommy danced and sniffed, shooting a glance up but someone came by laughing and then Justin took them toward the open doors of the huge master suite.

Gavin nudged her, his eyes moving down.

Brianne turned on the small landing to stare down into the crowd. A man dressed in black with dark hair and heavy brows stood near the entry hall, his back to them.

Tommy did his little dance again. And alerted.

But on who?

Brianne glanced around to Justin. He smiled and waited. "Ready to be wowed?"

"More than ready," she said.

Gavin took Tommy. "I think spoiled sport here is trying to tell me he needs to take a walk. I'll be right back." With that, he gave Brianne a quick kiss. "I'll hurry."

"Oh, you're so sweet to take care of my T-Boy," she said for Justin's benefit. "Is that our man?" she whispered against Gavin's ear.

"I think." He lifted away and spoke loudly. "I think I'll need another drink after we get back. You two behave."

Justin grinned like a Cheshire cat and twirled his expensive ring. "I'll take good care of her."

Brianne gave Justin a brilliant smile but wished she could follow Gavin and Tommy downstairs. Would Gavin be able to get close to that man?

Had they finally found the Tick at last?

"Find."

Tommy heard Gavin's one-word command when he whispered it. The dog knew hand signals enough to know they were officially on the case.

Tommy moved through the noisy crowd, pushing past people only to stop and turn back. The women thought he was adorable but they didn't bother to touch him. Just smiled and gave Gavin thorough come-hither gazes.

The men in the room focused on the chase—who would get this penthouse first. He heard snatches of Wall Street discussions, some rants on politics, the reviews of the latest musical on Broadway, the tall tales of a weekend in the Hamptons.

And while he listened and smiled and worked his way toward the elevator, he searched for the man in black with the heavy eyebrows. Where had he gone?

Gavin turned toward the kitchen where a white marble island covered with an array of food faced another city vista and the cabinets and appliances still smelled fresh and new. Tommy did a ground sniff and then lifted his head to a set of solid glass doors centered in a glass wall.

The terrace.

"Let's get some fresh air," Gavin said loud enough for anyone nearby to hear.

Taking Tommy out through the glass doors and into the heated dusk, he glanced around, admiring the view. But his eyes did a search of the entire terrace and the surrounding buildings. Up above, the master bedroom's ceiling-to-floor windows were covered in sheer curtains. Then he turned to the left, facing north toward Broadway. A door stood open at the other end of the penthouse.

"Let's try there," he said to Tommy.

The dog moved ahead with purpose. But when they reached the room, they found an empty office. *No one in here.*

The place shined with the same gray and white tones of the other rooms, with just a touch of red popping out. Tommy did a search, his nose hitting the lush white rug underneath the oval glass-topped desk. He lifted his snout to the gleaming white wood cabinets lined with artifacts and trinkets.

Tommy looked up before turning back to give Gavin a cue that meant he'd found something.

On the top of the massive built-in cabinets lay a plaid

baseball cap. Red, white and blue with a sparkling row of white gemstones across the rim.

"What?" Gavin asked the K-9. "Are you saying—"

"There you are."

Gavin turned to find Liza Collins smiling at him, her arms elegantly crossed over her white suit jacket. "Did you like the master?"

"Impressive," Gavin admitted, still wondering about that hat and this room. "T-Boy here needed some air. I was headed out the elevator but saw the terrace. The last rays of the sun slipping over it kind of drew me out there."

The woman's cool gaze moved from the sun-dappled terrace back to Gavin. "And yet, you're in here now."

"Yes, the door to the terrace was open."

She moved to close it. "Someone must have been in a hurry." Shutting the door, she turned back to Gavin. "It's still a bit warm out there."

Gavin noticed how the woman stood away from him and his partner. Maybe she didn't like big dogs.

Tommy did a little dance and lifted his snout. Had their man gotten away through the terrace doors? Gavin hadn't seen anyone on the terrace but Tommy had alerted on this room.

"Yes. I'm taking this one for his walk and then I'm going to find my wife and make sure she hasn't bought this place already."

"I'll see you back in the kitchen then," Liza said. But she turned and gave him one final glance. "I hope we can find what you're looking for, Mr. Reinhart. I hate to disappoint clients."

"From what Justin tells me, he knows how to make things happen," Gavin replied, wondering if she knew what her top salesman was really up to. Or if she cared.

"He's good at what he does," she said with an eloquent shrug. "I don't ask questions."

Did she have a clue or was she playing her own part in all of this? Gavin couldn't be sure.

He left her standing in the middle of the office and took Tommy down the elevator, hoping they'd pick up a scent.

But he had to wonder if Brianne was holding her own with Justin.

Gavin had a feeling she could do that with ease.

And he prayed she'd heed his warning and be careful.

Because right now, he had no idea what their next move would be.

Brianne didn't move. Justin had her cornered but she refused to be intimidated. The man had flirted, offered her wine and food, suggested they get together for lunch sometime and then practically begged her to buy this penthouse.

"Don't you think you'd rather live here?" he asked, his arms opening wide toward the view. "It's Tribeca after all. Some of the most sought-after property in all of Manhattan."

"I love this area," she admitted while she took in every detail of the room and this man. She couldn't see him as a bomber, however. He'd do the hiring but not the dirty work. "But as we've told you, we have a hands-on approach to buying properties. We've talked about Williamsburg—it's going through such a change these days. And, of course, we adore the Upper West Side and Central Park. But it seems everything old is going and all these new high-rises are appearing. I like to take old and make it new again, but the location is the thing. We need a good piece of property. Do you understand what I'm saying?"

"I make that kind of stuff happen," he said, moving closer. "I can find exactly what you want." His eyes danced over her with too much intimacy to suit Brianne. She held her spine tight so she wouldn't shudder.

"We're back."

They both whirled around to find Gavin standing there with Tommy. "And, Alice, darling, we're late for dinner." His gaze indicated they needed to hurry.

"Oh, well." She smiled at Justin. "Just when things were getting interesting. You will call us, right?"

"Of course," the real estate agent said, disappointment chilling his promise. "Don't worry. Soon we'll all have what we want." Then he shook Gavin's hand. "Good to see you again, Linus."

Gavin guided her down the stairs. "I got in a conversation with Morticia."

"Who?"

"Liza in the white suit. She reminds me of the matriarch of *The Addams Family*. Surely you watched that sitcom."

"Oh, her. Yes, I watched that show. This one is kind of creepy in a sophisticated way. That nickname fits her but I'll have to pull up all the news reports on her real life."

"Once I excused myself from her, I saw the man in black heading toward the elevator. If we hurry, we might catch him."

Keeping her voice low as they crossed the crowded room, she whispered, "Did Tommy alert?"

Gavin nodded. "I'll explain once we're out of here."

Brianne glanced back and saw Liza Collins watching them. "Morticia at your six."

"Keep walking," Gavin said. "I don't think she's our problem right now."

They didn't find their man in the elevator but Tommy seemed agitated, his snout in the air.

When they came out into the lobby, Gavin spotted their

man moving toward the front doors. Tommy went still and stared after him.

"Gotcha," Brianne said, hurrying with Gavin toward the front doors. But a crowd of laughing people pushed through, forcing them to wait.

When they got outside, Gavin saw the man disappearing around the corner. "Let's go," he said.

Brianne followed him into the dusk.

"What are we going to say when we get to him?" she asked.

Gavin gave her a quick glance. "I haven't gotten that far yet."

"If it's not him, Gavin, we'll blow our cover."

"Then we'll follow him and find out where he's headed."

Brianne nodded. "I believe Tommy and he seems to want to stay on this course."

"I agree," Gavin said, his stomach roiling. "I think we might have found our man but I need to see his face."

"You don't think he left anything back there, do you?" she asked.

"No bomb, but Tommy alerted on a plaid cap on a shelf in the bedroom, similar to the one the park bomber was wearing."

"I hope we can finally pin him down."

"I hope so, too," Gavin replied. "I want this to be the beginning of ending this thing."

Or…they'd been set up to chase someone who only wanted to lure them away and possibly kill them.

THIRTEEN

They tailed the man up Hudson for three blocks.

Gavin made sure they were well behind so he wouldn't notice. The man walked briskly, weaving in and out of people moving along the sidewalks, his stride purposeful. He never went inside any of the shops and he barely glanced around.

When he abruptly turned a corner to the right onto Leonard, Gavin grabbed Brianne to hide inside a doorway, his arms shielding her in case the man saw them when he whirled to the right.

Holding her there, Gavin stared down into her eyes, thinking he'd like to kiss her. Which was crazy and impossible right now. "That was close."

She nodded, her breath shallow, her gaze moving over his face. "You scared me."

"I thought he was turning back."

Tommy sat hidden with them and never uttered a sound.

Gavin checked the street on both sides. Nothing out of the ordinary along Hudson. "Let's go."

They turned the corner onto Leonard and Gavin spotted their suspect up ahead. Then Gavin slowed, careful to make it look like they were taking an evening stroll.

Then the man headed toward the subway station.

"Hurry," Gavin said, tugging Tommy along and holding Brianne's hand. "He's taking the Uptown 1 Line."

The man disappeared down the subway stairs.

Brianne rushed to keep up, but Gavin held her hand and

kept Tommy tight on his leash while they hurried down the stairs to the train platform. "There," she whispered.

They saw the man moving through the crowd waiting for the next train, his head down and turned away.

Gavin found a spot next to a support column, mindful of keeping out of sight.

When the incoming train arrived, a mob of passengers started disembarking. The man shoved through people still trying to exit, knocking them out of his way as he squeezed through the train doors. By the time they'd reached the doors of the train, the man had barreled through the crowds inside, his face disappearing in a crush of commuters and tourists. They made the door just as it shut, leaving them standing on the platform.

"I don't see him anymore," Brianne said.

Gavin tried to find the man. "We can't get to him. Even if we'd made the train, he'd have spotted us."

"So that's it?" Brianne asked, her tone full of aggravation.

"For now," Gavin said, feeling the same. "We can't halt the train without a warrant or order from someone higher up. We've got nothing to go on but a scent and a description."

"He might have made us. The way he hurried onto that train shows he's up to something."

Gavin let out a sigh. "I don't think he saw us but yes, he could be in a hurry for a reason."

"I hope that reason has nothing to do with us." She didn't look so sure.

"No, I watched. He never turned his head," Gavin replied as they pivoted to walk back to the Bec-Off-Broadway. "I don't think he spotted us."

"Or he could have been pretending," Brianne pointed

out. "If he's the Tick, he'd know how to blend into a crowd and he'd know the busiest subway lines this time of day."

"Good point," Gavin said, aggravation coloring his words.

"It's a start," Brianne said as they walked back the way they'd come. "Our hands are tied, Gavin. We can't do much more without bringing in actual detectives."

"I think it's time we did that," he said, hating to admit it. "We're out of our league and…we still need to chase leads on Jordan's murderer. Not to mention, we have patrol duties in various other places."

They were almost back to the valet station when Brianne stopped and stared at a flyer on the window of an art gallery.

"Look, Gavin. 'Dog Days of Tribeca.' At the Washington Market Park this weekend."

"What does that have to do with us?" he asked, tired and irritated.

"Sponsored by the Realtors of Rexx."

That got Gavin's attention. "Interesting. Trying to impress the neighbors?"

"Neighbors with dogs," Brianne replied. "We have dogs. We saw a lot of people there tonight with dogs. Maybe we can snoop around a little bit and spot some of the other brokers we saw there tonight."

"Another walk in the park," Gavin said. "It sure can't hurt."

"Linus and Alice strike again," she said, smiling now.

"Okay, I'll pick you up—"

"Not at the safe house. It'll take far less time for me to get ready at home and take the subway directly to Tribeca."

"How about we meet near the park? There's another garage between Greenwich and Reade," Gavin said.

She nodded. "I'll text you, so we can walk out of the garage together."

"Okay, but be careful."

"Always," she said.

The valet went to the parking garage around the corner to find their car. Gavin glanced around out of habit. No one watching or lurking about. But Tommy's head went up as they waited at the entryway of the apartment building.

"Bree, we've got something."

Tommy sniffed the air, but the dog faced away from the building and looked to the left.

To the parking garage.

"I hear you," Brianne said. "Let's see where Tommy takes us."

"Go. Find." Gavin's word weren't out before Tommy took off into the garage. "He's following the same route as the valet."

"The valet? I can't believe he'd be involved in this."

"I can," Gavin replied. "Anyone here today could be involved. Money makes people do strange things. Maybe we've been following the wrong man."

They reached the exit from the garage when Gavin saw the parking attendant bringing back their luxury sedan.

Waving the man down, Gavin stopped him at the entryway.

"Maybe he picked up something on the street or in the garage," Brianne said, determination clear in her words. They hurried to meet the man.

Tommy barked and tried to move forward toward the car. "Let's see." Gavin held Tommy back. "He'll let us know if something's not right with this attendant"

The young attendant got out, standing with the car door open, confusion clouding his face, but Tommy ignored him.

Gavin came up with an excuse. "We thought we'd save you some trouble, so we strolled up the block. Our dog is restless."

The man nodded and shrugged, but he started toward Gavin. "Whatever, man."

Tommy zoomed in on the car and kept tugging.

"He's alerting on the car, not the man," Gavin whispered, giving Brianne a surprised frown.

The attendant was about ten feet from where he'd left the car running and pulled up just inside the exit. Tommy pivoted to Gavin and whirled back to stare at the car.

Gavin shouted, "Run. Get away from that car!"

The kid looked up, surprised. He stopped and looked back.

"Hurry!"

Gavin jumped into action and hurled himself toward Brianne and pulled her back, Tommy going with them as they ducked behind a wide concrete and steel pillar.

Before the valet could move, a loud boom hit the night air, echoing against the buildings all around.

Shrapnel flew out through the air, dinging and sputtering against parked cars on the street and hitting the windows of nearby buildings. Gavin felt a sharp, searing pain near his right temple. Brianne gasped and ducked her head, her arms going over Tommy to shield the dog.

Then the place went silent.

Gavin jumped up and dropped Tommy's leash, then took off running to where the unconscious valet attendant lay near the burning wreckage of the car, dark smoke surrounding them.

With a grunt and a tug, he pulled the bleeding man away from the destroyed car. Through the buzz in his ears, Gavin heard Brianne calling in their location and giving directions to the 911 dispatcher.

"Hurry," she shouted into her cell phone. "The vehicle could start leaking fumes."

Then she ordered Tommy to stay and ran toward Gavin and the injured attendant. Grabbing the man's legs, she helped Gavin move him off to the side, out of danger from the still-burning car and out of the path of any vehicles that might emerge around the corner. Alarms were going off everywhere. People came running. Cars skidded to a stop.

Gavin worked on keeping the man alive, checking his pulse and giving him chest compressions.

Brianne looked up and into Gavin's eyes. "I guess we won't be using the fancy car again."

"Nope." He turned his head to scan the area. "And we need to get out of here before everyone comes down to see what happened. We don't want Sanelli or Liza Collins to see us here."

Brianne stared up at the building down the street. "They won't like this kind of publicity."

Then she saw the blood running down his face near his left eye. "Gavin, you're hurt."

"Tell me about it. Burning like a bed of ants attacking me."

"You need help," she said, trying to reach out.

"No, *he* needs help. We'll worry about me later." Then he checked her over. "Are you all right?"

"I'm good," she said. "And so is our partner."

Gavin nodded and went back to counting compressions.

"I've got a pulse," he said.

By then, the first responders had arrived and someone moved them out of the way so they could get to work on saving the young attendant while the fire department put out the vehicle fire. After showing the first responders their IDs, Gavin and Brianne watched from a distance, careful to stay hidden inside one of the squad cars that had responded. Soon the firemen had the burning vehicle hosed down. Since the car had been in front of the building and away from most of the other parked cars, they were able to contain the explosion.

Gavin grabbed one of the firemen. "What's the status?"

"We haven't located the source yet, but I'd say a small incendiary device, probably triggered remotely. Could have been a lot worse. If it had exploded inside the garage and caused the gas tank to leak, the gas fumes probably would have ignited this whole place."

Brianne took Gavin farther away, around the corner and out of sight. "We need to get that gash on your temple checked."

"I'm fine," he growled, not used to being pampered. Then he looked into her eyes. "This is my fault, Brianne. If that boy dies, it's on me."

"No, it's not," she argued. "You know who did this. The Tick. He must have doubled back to leave an explosive on our car."

"I brought the car here."

"But you didn't place that bomb on it. You do realize he wants us dead?"

"I do, yes. That's why I'm so mad right now."

Brianne took his hand. "Don't be mad. We have to get even. Now we have proof someone is trying to kill us, Gavin. This is the third time, at that."

"And it won't be the last," he finally said. "Are you willing to stay with me until the end, Brianne?"

"I want you both off this case," Noah said when the whole team had gathered in the conference room the next morning. Noah explained the situation, bringing some surprised grunts and glares from several people.

"But, sir, we're so close," Gavin said, shooting a glance at Brianne. "We have to finish this thing."

"We can't stop searching now, sir," she echoed, frustration scraping across her frazzled system.

"He blew up your car," Noah reminded them. "No, wait, he blew up a car Gavin rented from a friend."

"A friend who has good insurance since he deals in luxury rentals."

"I'm not worried about insurance on the car," Noah replied, his tone hitting Brianne like nails on tin. "You two have been threatened enough and we're thankful that the attendant survived and is okay. I'm bringing in detectives for backup and I'm ordering you both to take it easy for the rest of the week." Glaring at them, he tossed them a stack of files. "See what you can find on the details of my brother's death."

"Desk duty?" Gavin said, anger coloring his words.

Brianne shot him a warning glance. "Good idea, sir. Things are too hot right now."

"Agreed," Noah replied, glancing around at the other officers. "Now…let's get to work. And you two, in my office so we can talk about how to proceed when you turn this case over to the detectives."

Gavin and Brianne exchanged looks. He wouldn't want to let go of the Tick. She'd promised to stand by him. Somebody needed to have his back.

Once they were inside Noah's office with the door shut, Brianne and Gavin sat down and waited for Noah to let them have it. Instead, he stared out the window.

"Sir?"

"I know, I know," Noah said. "You want to stay on this. You're close to finding a possible bomber. But…we don't know if this is the work of the Fourth of July bomber or the Tick, do we? Or if they are both the same man."

"I'll get on the lab to get DNA results," Gavin said.

"And I'll see if they found any trace evidence on Scrawny," Brianne added.

Noah's eyebrows shot up. "Scrawny?"

"The mutt we found at the building site the other day," Brianne said. "We think the person who shoved the beam had been with the dog before. The way the dog acted and sniffed the air made me think he caught the man's scent." Her hands on the arms of her chair, she added, "We might find some trace evidence on the dog—human hair, epidermis, fibers, anything."

"And that person could be one of our alleged bombers?"

"Yes, sir." Brianne nodded. "Or…it's not connected and just someone who doesn't want us to find your brother's killer."

"None of this makes sense," Noah admitted. "I had my doubts about letting you two do this on your own since you're not trained in undercover work and now I'll hear it from everyone up the chain of command. As if I don't have enough to deal with."

"We don't mind bringing in a couple of detectives, sir," Gavin replied. "I wanted to talk to you about that very thing."

"Well, that's something to be glad about," Noah said before sitting back in his chair.

Gavin went over their plan again. "We need to meet with Justin Sanelli one more time and seal the deal. That means we'd have to make a huge down payment on the property we pick—if we get that far."

"If these people are on to you, how do you plan to do that?"

Brianne sat up straight. "If we get in, we can possibly catch the bomber in the act. Set up a sting."

"You'll need help with that."

"We agree," she said, daring Gavin to argue with her.

Noah tapped his fingers on his calendar pad. "The commissioner's not happy about the car exploding but I assured him you are both all right and the City of New York will not be held accountable. The fire department managed to contain the fire to that vehicle. Not much damage but we'll have to pay for a few repairs on the parking garage."

"We need one more try, sir," Gavin said.

"So you think this bomber is working on his own, or with one of the brokers?"

"We don't know. We're trying to follow the information and piece things together, but we think Justin Sanelli could be involved. He could have distracted us at the open house while the bomber found our car. Tommy alerted at the open house and we tracked the man we believe to be the bomber until he got onto the subway.

Noah rubbed his chin. "So you think the man you saw at the open house watched you two arrive and slipped into the garage to plant the bomb?

They both nodded. "Or he took us on a merry chase so someone else could plant the explosives," Gavin said.

"Did anyone see you after the car exploded?"

"Not that we know of," Brianne replied. "We waited for backup and showed our IDs, then went around the corner. We didn't mingle with the crowd."

Noah studied his notes. "And we still can't find this William Caston who Brianne ID'd as the possible Fourth of July bomber. Did you get a look at the face of the man you followed today? Could he be the Tick?"

"We don't know, sir," Brianne said, shaking her head. "We never saw his face. We need solid evidence."

Noah sat silent for a minute. "Desk duty until the weekend, then come back with a plan, including discussing this with the detectives on Monday, okay? You're not going out on this again without sufficient backup, understood?"

"Understood," they both said in unison.

Once they were out and about and going to their desks to dig into files, Brianne turned to Gavin. "What about the park on Saturday?"

He gave her a solemn glance. "Nothing says we can't go to the park, Bree, and take our dog for a walk."

"As Linus and Alice?"

"No, but disguised. Hats, sunshades and whatever else will make us look like normal people. We'll stay on the fringes of the crowd."

"Okay, I'll bring Stella since they might recognize Tommy. No one knows her and it'll be a good teachable moment for her. But, Gavin, normal is not in my vocabulary."

"I'm beginning to see that," he replied before he turned to his cubicle. The red welt on his temple reminded her of how close they'd come to being blown to smithereens.

But did he see everything? she wondered. Did he see the truth of her feelings each time he looked into her eyes?

FOURTEEN

"So we're doing this?"

Gavin glanced over at Brianne after they met up in the designated spot, glad to see she was okay after two days of being tied to her desk and the training yard.

Brushing her fingers through Stella's shining golden coat, she said, "Sure, Sutherland, let's go have some fun."

Gavin pivoted to get a good look at her. They'd both changed up their looks yet again. "Aren't you glad to be out in the fresh air on a Saturday morning?"

"You know I'm grumpy in the mornings," she quipped. "Especially when I'm chasing after an elusive bomber in the middle of New York."

They stopped on the street, their eyes meeting.

For a brief moment, the noise of traffic and sirens and planes overhead, the sound of honking horns, children laughing and dogs barking—all of the things that made up New York City—went out of his head.

And he saw her. Only her.

He'd like to see her every morning, just like this. Grumpy or not.

He'd never been able to keep the world away, to be so calm and sure that he could focus on one thing and one thing only. Even when he worked, Gavin's mind worked along with him, like a roller coaster that couldn't stop running. Granny Irene used to tell him to focus and he'd learned how to do that on most days. But he always had a hard time trying to find complete calm and peace.

But with Brianne he felt calm and secure, although he worried about protecting her, even when the world seemed to be closing in on him.

"Gavin?"

"What?"

"Why are you staring at me like that?"

"I don't know. How is *like that*?"

Her eyes went dark with awareness. "As if we're still Linus and Alice and you'd like to kiss me."

"I'm not Linus right now, Bree. But yes, I am thinking about kissing you."

She backed away, causing Stella to give them a surprised stare. "That would be stupid."

She always made him laugh.

"You're something, you know that?"

"I'm your partner and we're walking a thin line with the entire police department. Yesterday, I had a quick lunch with Lani and Faith. They grilled me about us. People are talking."

"People are always talking."

"Stop flirting with me."

"You think I'm flirting? Really?"

"You said you wanted to kiss me."

"I'm being honest. I'd have to be dead not to notice you."

Today, she wore torn jeans and a high-necked sleeveless white blouse covered with rows of colorful necklaces and chains, a pair of strappy tan sandals and a big floral tote bag with a pair of black sunshades peeking out of a side pocket. A pretty blue scarf covered her messy now-red-again bun.

"Well, stick with me and we could both be dead," she replied with her sarcasm intact. "Each time I'm around you, someone tries to kill me."

"Bree, I'm being serious."

"I can see that. But aren't we here for pretend fun?"

He didn't understand why she tried to push him away. She'd said she didn't want any tangled relationships and he'd felt the same at first. Maybe he needed to grasp that and get back to work. Or it could be that she sensed that unease that covered him like an aura. He'd never fit in with her world because he didn't know how to do family stuff or people stuff. Always a loner. Always waiting and wondering and asking himself why he'd been abandoned by his own mother.

Would he ever be able to let go and just live, really live?

He needed to talk to the Big Man upstairs about that. Ask for some guidance on getting his life right before he turned into a perpetual bachelor.

He'd always felt the same way about work as she did— all business and no time for a love life—until he'd asked her to be his pretend wife. Dangerous territory.

Focus.

"Fun it is," he retorted, tamping down his anger and his awareness. "Fun while we try to find a bomber and his boss."

"Now that's my kind of Saturday at the park," she said, grabbing him by the arm. "Let's go explore the farmer's market and then we'll let Stella run with the big dogs."

Gavin shook his head and followed her. Her brave, carefree nature always amazed him. And scared him. He could take care of himself. He'd been doing that for years. He could be ruthless and daring. He'd learned that in high school and had come close to a crash-and-burn. But Granny Irene had nipped that in the bud by getting him a part-time job as an orderly at the hospital.

Seeing the ER on Saturdays had made him choose the law enforcement path where he'd learned to be cautious and conscientious. But the driving need to help people had carried him through.

Brianne seemed to thrive on being relentless, a good trait, but sometimes being concise and sure could win the day.

Which left him trying to figure out how to protect a woman who had too much gumption for her own good.

Well that was the thing—she'd warned him over and that she truly didn't want a man trying to protect her.

Or maybe at least not this man.

She'd wanted that kiss.

Brianne realized, while she hid behind her sunglasses and browsed through a booth full of colorful Bohemian clothes, she might be pretending a lot lately, but she'd been serious when she'd stared into Gavin's eyes an hour ago. It would have been so easy to give in, but she'd been burned by being too impulsive with her last boyfriend and too trusting with her best friend. They'd gone off together and done a number on her.

Burned and hurt and disillusioned. She charged ahead in life, but not in her love life. Not anymore.

Being a part of this case could make or break her career in law enforcement and she wasn't letting up now. She was too deep into pretending on so many levels.

It was one thing to pretend because of an undercover operation but quite another to pretend she didn't have feelings for Gavin Sutherland. She refused to let those feeling get in the way of keeping him safe and bringing in a domestic terrorist.

She had to stay the course and maybe, later, they could revisit a possible kiss. In the meantime, she would hold tight to the memory of his eyes filled with hope and passion and awareness. She'd hold on to that moment they'd shared, with the world so alive and colorful and brimming with possibilities all around them, while they were just two people fighting the good fight and fighting their own battle to keep away from each other.

"Hey, you okay?"

Brianne looked up and saw Gavin through her sunglasses. "Yes, just trying to decide if I need this tunic." Holding up the colorful, sleeveless cotton garment, she asked, "What do you think?"

He smiled and did another scan of their surroundings. "I think it's time to make our rounds."

Brianne paid the older woman manning the booth the twenty dollars for the tunic. A keepsake, colorful and bursting with life, to remind her of being in the park with Gavin.

After tucking the paper bag holding the tunic into her tote, she checked the gun nestled in the side pocket hidden inside.

Gavin wore a NY Yankees cap and dark shades, an old faded T-shirt and worn jeans, a five-o'clock shadow giving him a rugged look. He looked good and blended in with the crowd. She tried to do the same. She could pretend they were a couple strolling through the park while Stella sniffed and worked her scent grid.

When they reached a spot near the big overhead banner close to the gazebo that read Welcome to the Dog Days of Washington Market Park, sponsored by the Realtors of Rexx, she glanced around and immediately spotted Liza Collins standing near a table holding a tiny Yorkie in her arms. Liza wore crisp white jeans and a black-and-white striped cotton T-shirt, her sandals tall-heeled and expensive-looking, her Wayfarers black and dark. The tiny dog yelped and put on a fierce front despite the pink bow around her little neck.

"Gavin."

"I see. We can't get too close."

"Okay, so we stroll around the perimeters and keep our eyes open."

"Yes, and our ears. We might hear tidbits here and there."

"I don't think she'll notice us. It's getting pretty crowded."

People with their dogs were everywhere. Several booths touting dog food and chew toys were set up along the tree line, offering everything from treats to comfortable doggie beds to demonstrations on how to exercise and train animals or keep them calm during storms and other traumatic events.

"Quite an array of interesting products," she whispered close, hoping no one noticed them.

"Yeah." Gavin laughed as if he didn't have a care in the world. "You'd think people would figure out dogs only need love and a chew toy."

"That's a good start."

"Maybe that's all people need, too. To be loved and to have something or someone to comfort them and make them feel useful."

Her heart did that strange bump. The one that made her want to pull him close and hold him tight to show him he had someone on his side. "Listen to you, oh, wise one."

"I'm learning," he said, his smile soft and real. "I'm a loner but I could get used to this."

Stella halted and sniffed the air, then looked toward the big information booth.

Brianne glanced over to where Liza stood talking to a group of people. "Gavin, check it out."

Gavin looked over. One guy shifted his position, and Gavin froze. "Well, would you look at that?"

The Bushy-Brows Man. The one they'd followed into the subway and lost.

The Tick—maybe.

"The guy from last night! And he's talking to Morticia."

Gavin nodded. "And Stella recognizes him."

"She smells his scent, even if he's not carrying a bomb. Or is he?"

"I don't think the man would bomb this park. He looks too chummy with Liza."

Brianne took out her cell and snapped away, being careful to get pictures of the scenery while taking in the crowd. But she got two close-up shots of Liza with Bushy-Brows Man.

"William Caston?" she asked, her voice low and steady. "Sure looks like the mugshot."

"My gut says yes—and that he's the Tick," he replied. "We should have lab reports next week. We need a connection to that man and the Fourth of July bomber. Something to indicate they're one and the same guy."

"And now, we need to find out more on Liza Collins, too," Brianne said. "She made a big deal out of her husband's death. Blamed other brokers for the stress that caused his heart attack."

They strolled as close as they could get without being obvious. Brianne watched the people gathered around the information table. Justin Sanelli was nowhere to be found but Liza definitely worked the crowd. And the Bushy-Brows Man seemed to follow her around, listening and watching.

"Maybe he's her bodyguard," she said to Gavin.

"Then why did he abandon her at the open house and take us on a merry chase the other night?"

"To protect her," Brianne said. "Maybe just like with

our suspicions about the Fourth of July bombing, that man could be a decoy and a distraction. But we still don't know if he deliberately tried to lead us away after he placed a bomb on the car or if he was just leaving the open house while someone else placed that device in our car."

Gavin gave her a nod. "I'm beginning to see the logic in him being a decoy." Glaring at Liza through his dark shades, he added, "And I'm wondering if she's the one calling the shots."

"Now we just have to follow the evidence and prove that theory," she replied.

Gavin and Brianne did hear tidbits of conversations while they strolled around the event.

"Yes, we just moved to Chelsea. Love the quaintness of the neighborhood."

"No, we decided against the efficiency in Midtown. The association wanted too much personal information."

"Yes, I talked to Justin just the other day. It's a go on the Central Park West property. Justin says things will get moving there very soon. I can't wait to see what he does with the place."

Brianne and Gavin smiled and spoke to people, talking about dogs in general, but stayed toward the back of the crowd. Bushy-Brows Man shadowed Morticia and her overly excited dog. They never once looked toward Brianne and Gavin.

"I think we should go," Gavin whispered, his head almost touching hers. "We need to find out more about Liza."

"I agree," she said after they'd ordered some iced tea from a coffee shop near the park. "At least we've established that Bushy-Brows is a dead-ringer for the Fourth of July bomber."

"And that he is highly involved with the Rexx Agency. Which supports our theory that both bombers are one and the same."

"Okay," she said as they scrolled back to the parking garage. "Let's take him in for questioning."

"Not yet," he replied. "We need to form a plan to finish this. We need to do as Noah told us and set up a sting. Besides, we're not here officially."

"Why don't we catalog this and talk about Jordan's death? What are we all missing there?"

"I don't know," he said. "We've been helping the team follow leads for months now and the only thing we've come close to was possibly finding Snapper, as if that could give us any answers. That turned out to be another setup or maybe something else to taunt us."

"We know a thug named Claude Jenks planted the suicide note and now he's dead," Brianne said as they entered the parking garage. "He can't tell us who hired him."

"We've gone over the woods where Jordan was found and didn't find much there to go on, either."

"I hope the lab techs can find something on Scrawny, so we can figure out if Jordan's killer planted the dog there to mess with part of the team or if our bomber is responsible."

Gavin guided her toward where he'd parked on the second level, using his personal vehicle today.

When he went to unlock it, Brianne stopped him. "Wait, Gavin. Let Stella get in some practice."

She guided the dog to the car and commanded Stella to search. The big girl worked her way around the car, sniffing and lowering her snout to the garage floor and then lifting her head to sniff the air and the vehicle's exterior. When she didn't find anything, Brianne breathed a sigh of relief.

"We're clear."

Then they heard footsteps hitting hard against concrete.

Someone came running toward them.

FIFTEEN

Gavin grabbed Brianne and tugged her away from the plain tan SUV. Commanding "Quiet" to Stella through a hand signal, he quickly moved them three cars away and pushed Brianne down behind a huge pickup truck.

The footsteps slowed, moving with a light tap that hit the concrete with an eerie cadence, grating against Gavin's nerves. He held his breath while he kept Brianne and the K-9 out of sight. Was someone lost? Or searching for them?

Brianne lifted her weapon out of her tote bag, checked the magazine and nodded to him. Stella sat attentive but didn't make a sound.

Gavin silently thanked God that Brianne and Lani were such dedicated K-9 officers. Stella proved to be as good as Tommy at following orders and sniffing out bombs.

He held a finger to his lips as he stayed low and took a quick glance around the truck's heavy grill. Then he held up one finger to Brianne to indicate he only saw one person.

A man moving from car to car. When the stranger came up on Gavin's SUV, he stopped and stared at the vehicle.

Gavin held his breath. He waited, held back and watched, fully expecting the man to plant a bomb or place a tracker on the SUV.

The man leaned over and stared inside the locked car. Gavin noticed he held something in one hand but he couldn't surmise whether it was a weapon or a phone. The man glanced around, but he wore dark shades and stayed in the shadows. After a moment, he turned back and studied the vehicle again. Then he squatted near the front driver's side tire.

When a nearby vehicle cranked and started backing out, the man whirled and disappeared back toward the garage stairs and took off down toward the first floor.

The other car drove around, exiting the garage, the driver unaware that he'd probably just stopped a crime.

"Stay here," Gavin told Brianne on a curt whisper.

Her eyebrows slanted up, the questioning expression telling him she didn't like that command.

But Gavin didn't stop to argue with her. He stood but stayed low, the weapon he'd hidden at his waist now in his hand, and trotted toward where the man had gone down the stairs. Gavin leaned over the railing by the street and glanced below to the stairs and the sidewalk. But he didn't see anyone lurking about and no one left or right on the street who matched the person he'd seen earlier.

Families with laughing children, a couple walking hand in hand, an older woman pushing a stroller.

Gavin studied all of them, looking for the man who'd been too interested in his vehicle. The old woman with the stroller looked a little off. Gavin watched, waiting.

But the old woman turned and greeted a younger woman. They hugged and the older woman lifted a beautiful baby out of the stroller and handed the little girl, all dressed in pink, to the woman who was obviously her mother.

Pushing away the pangs of anger and hurt that image brought out, Gavin hit the railing and turned to hurry back to Brianne and their partner.

Once again, the bomber had come and gone. If that had been the bomber. Hard to tell in the dark muted lights of the parking garage if he'd actually left something on the SUV.

Frustrated, Gavin headed back to the spot where he'd left Brianne and Stella.

But she wasn't waiting there.

Brianne did yet another sweep of the garage, her eyes adjusting to the dark hot place while she watched Stella going over Gavin's vehicle for the third time.

If that man had planted anything, Stella would sniff it out. But she sniffed the ground around the SUV and kept moving, trying to follow the stranger's scent out onto the street below. Brianne had checked the tires and hadn't found any kind of damage there. What had that guy been doing? Would she suspect everyone for the rest of her life and chalk it up to being a police officer?

When she heard footsteps and realized someone was approaching, she signaled Stella back and raised her weapon.

Only to find Gavin rushing toward her.

"What are you doing?" he asked, clearly out of breath.

"I'm checking your vehicle for bombs or trackers," she explained. "Did you find anyone?"

"No. Gone. Again."

So he wasn't in a good mood and why should she blame him? "Well, your SUV is clear. I've searched it thoroughly."

"I told you to stay behind the truck."

The man was seriously stubborn in the protection detail department. She didn't need a detail or his protection and while it touched her each time he tried to take care of her, it also irritated her to no end. But she'd let that slide for now.

"I'm a cop, Gavin. I'm just as capable as you in checking out this scene."

He let out a sigh and shook his head. "Yes, you are. I overreacted."

"But you're still not happy with me."

"You're still a rookie."

Brianne couldn't believe he'd just said that. "Gavin? Honestly?"

"I'm sorry, Bree. But you need to learn to follow procedure."

"Follow procedure? I did follow procedure. I took our bomb-sniffing K-9 to a site that I thought might have been compromised. Your personal vehicle. What if the bomb had gone off?"

He stared into her eyes and then looked out toward the street. "Okay, all right. I'm frustrated because I don't know what's going on. Is the bomber following us? Or does this have something to do with Jordan's death? I want things resolved."

"We all do," she said, changing her tone from defensive to accepting. "But we have to work the cases as they come. You know that. We get called out every day on nothing cases and now we've got two major ones going on. It's hard and it's stressful and none of us have had time to grieve for Jordan."

He placed his hands on his hips and gave her a softer stare. "I'm sorry. That rookie comment was uncalled-for. You've gone above and beyond."

"Yes, it sure was and yes, I've tried. You're welcome, by the way."

"For?"

"For me making sure you didn't get blown to pieces just now."

He actually cracked a smile. "Thank you, Bree, for doing your job."

"And thank you, Gavin, for trying to protect your team.

But we are a team, right? We work in tandem to get things taken care of and sometimes that means we have to break a few rules."

"As long as breaking the rules keeps you safe and sound and is within the guidelines."

"I'll do my best on that."

He glanced around again and then leaned close. "Bree, I'm a pain. I know that. But…you're one of the few people in our unit who seems to trust me enough to work with me. I won't forget that. I won't forget you."

"I don't want you to forget me," she said, wishing she could let go and tell him how she really felt. But he couldn't know that her feelings for him were changing and growing deeper every day. "I won't let you forget me, Gavin."

He nodded, but neither of them spoke, that silent but swift undercurrent charging through them and bonding them in a way no words of explanation ever could.

Finally, he said, "Okay, we made progress today, at least. We've got some homework to do."

Yes, they'd made progress on the case. But with each other? Still at a standoff point.

"I'm going do some digging on Liza Collins and I want to talk to Violet again tonight," she replied. "See if they've had any more brokers trying to get her and her parents to sell Griffin's."

"Good. I've tried to pin her down but she's either on her way to work at the airport or on her way to help out at the diner. She told me again she'd seen a couple of real estate brokers talking to her dad but said it all seemed civil and there was no pressure."

"Maybe the brokers seemed that way but we know different," Brianne replied. "She might be more willing to talk to me."

"Why? Because you're not as uptight and gruff as me?"

"Something like that, yeah."

His grin caught Brianne and took the breath right out of her lungs. The man really should smile more often.

Hitting the key fob to let Stella in the back, he looked over at her again. "I'll pester the lab until we get something on the Fourth of July bomber—anything that can tie him to the Tick. I can't find Beanpole. I'm beginning to worry that he's skipped town."

"You can drop Stella and me at the nearest subway station," Brianne said once they were in the SUV.

"No way. It's our day off, Brianne. I'm taking you home."

"You're not gonna do a sweep of my house again, are you?"

"Maybe. Just to be sure."

"Gavin…"

"Bree, humor me, okay."

"Would you do that if I were Carter or Finn?"

"No, but they're not nearly as pretty as you."

"I think you like being at my house. Pizza, hamburgers and now giving me a ride home."

"Maybe it's not the house I like, but the woman who lives there."

That remark flowed over her, warming her in a way that she hadn't experienced before. He did make her feel safe and secure. But this kind of security had nothing to do with bad guys or tracking explosive devices. This security had to do with her heart and how she needed to keep it safe.

Gavin might just be the one man who could give her that kind of security. Giving in to that feeling, she said, "Okay, big guy. You can come in and explore to your heart's desire."

He nodded, clearly pleased with himself. "Good. That's good, Bree. I feel better already."

Brianne decided Gavin needed to feel secure. And he needed to make others feel secure.

Her parents had given her security and a good home. She always felt safe with her parents around.

He'd never had that kind of security growing up—not the kind she'd had with two loving parents. His mother had abandoned him and his grandmother, while providing him with the necessary things he needed, had obviously tried to show her love for him in the most practical of ways.

But had she forgotten to show a scared, confused little boy the kind of emotional love that all humans craved?

Brianne said a little prayer for her big hunky partner while they traveled across the city. She didn't mind the bumper-to-bumper traffic or the long commute. From now on, she'd try to appreciate him more. That's what the man needed—respect and appreciation.

She could show him that, at least. High time someone did.

They talked. Really talked. About New York, about why they both became police officers.

"So you have different reasons than me," she said.

Gavin checked the GPS for the quickest route and took a bridge across the river.

"Yes." The heavy traffic moved at a brisk pace. "My grandfather died in a horrible wreck. He worked in Manhattan and made a good living. My grandmother often talked about how busy the city could be. She admired the police department. She encouraged me to be of service, so she got me a job working with her in the ER. I mean, she was a hardworking nurse who saw the underbelly of all of New York. I got a good look at that, too, working in a hospital during my last year of high school."

"But you didn't become a nurse or a doctor."

"No, I wanted to be a cop. I watched police roaming

the halls, filing reports, holding down meth addicts, some bringing tough-as-nails K-9s with them. I was hooked."

"My daddy would talk about the people we never notice when he'd describe his day to me," Brianne admitted. "He always had praise for law enforcement. I think they both influenced us in their own way."

"Sounds so," he replied. "I loved animals, but Granny didn't want a dog in the house. Too much trouble. I finally convinced her to let me get one when I mentioned I wanted to become a K-9 officer. She seemed impressed when I trained a mutt from the city pound by myself."

"I always had a pet," Brianne said, holding a hand on the dash when they came off the bridge to follow 287 into Queens. "I tormented them into being trained, too." Then she laughed. "My mom has a tiny Chihuahua. Serpico is fierce. He sleeps with Stella and me and travels with them."

"We are a pair."

When they finally pulled up at Brianne's house, she noticed the door to the one-car garage stood open.

"That's odd. I know that door was down when I left. We never open it since we don't park in there."

"All the more reason for me to go inside the house with you," Gavin said, putting the SUV into Park and hurrying around to let Stella out. Giving the Quiet signal, he met Brianne as she slid out of her seat.

Slowly, they made their way to the open garage and moved around boxes of Christmas decorations and pieces of old furniture until they'd made it to the door leading to the kitchen.

Gavin went first, and Brianne didn't argue with him. Someone was clearly inside since they heard pots and pans banging.

"On three," Gavin said, waiting for Brianne to open the door so he could charge in.

He counted and she followed his lead, grabbing the doorknob to slam back the door.

Gavin rushed toward the door Stella on his heels.

Brianne followed. Then he heard a loud scream followed by an agonizing male groan and several sharp yelps and Stella's excited barks. Brianne went into action, her weapon drawn.

But the scene she saw in the kitchen stopped her cold.

SIXTEEN

Her mother stood holding a frying pan up in a defensive mode.

Serpico yelped and bared his teeth while he danced in a ranting circle, his short light-brown fur on edge.

Gavin stood by a happy-barking Stella, both of them wide-eyed, holding his weapon down.

Stella stopped short and then yelped at seeing her little friend. Serpico yelped back, but trembled in place.

Gavin rubbed his right shoulder. "Your mom knows how to use that frying pan."

Brianne took one look at the scene and burst out laughing.

"What is so funny?" her frightened mother asked, still holding the frying pan.

"I'm wondering that myself," Gavin added. Then he glanced at her mom. "May I put my weapon away?"

Her mother nodded, slowly. "Yes, and I shall do the same."

They both stared at each other while Gavin put his gun back underneath his T-shirt and her mother lowered the ridiculously huge frying pan onto the counter.

Stella sniffed. Gavin blushed. Serpico snarled. Her mother didn't move.

Brianne pushed past Gavin. "Serpico, hush up. Mom, are you all right?"

"Other than having my nineteenth heart attack, I am perfectly fine," her mother said, her salt-and-pepper short hair seeming to stand straight up on her head. "Who is this man?"

"I'm Gavin Sutherland," Gavin said, offering his hand in peace. "I work with Brianne."

"Officer," her mother replied, taking his hand with all the grace of a queen. "Nice to meet you."

"Same here, ma'am," Gavin said.

"Gavin, this is my mother, Janet Hayes," Brianne said, still smiling.

Gavin nodded and dropped her mother's hand. "I'm sorry for startling you."

"I'm fine," Mom said. "My heart rate is going down, at least." Then she glanced at his shoulder. "I've assaulted a police officer. I'm sorry."

Motioning to Serpico, Janet watched him trot over and then lifted the little imp up and soothed him with soft words. Serpico shot Gavin a petulant pout, followed by another snarl, his little body shaking despite his bravado.

Brianne knew she'd have some explaining to do. But first she had some questions. "Mom, I didn't know you and Dad were coming home today. Where's your car?"

"Your father went to get milk and eggs," Mom said, waving her hand in the air. "I told him that could wait. And I did try to call you. Many times."

Brianne winced. "I had my phone muted for part of the day."

"Oh, well, that explains it," her mother said with that infamous tone Brianne knew so well. Then she put Serpico down and told him to find his bed. The little fellow tapped across the room and hopped up onto his tiny doggie bed, his big brown eyes daring anyone to mess with him.

"We were on a case, Mrs. Hayes," Gavin said, clearly respectful of that frying pan. "It's my fault. I told her to silence her phone."

"And she listened?"

Now Gavin burst out laughing. "For once, yes," he said.

"You'll stay for dinner, then." her mother replied, not really forming it as a question.

Gavin glanced at Brianne, his body language shouting panic.

"Mom, Gavin was just dropping me off."

"Nonsense," her petite mother retorted, pulling things out of the refrigerator. "I'll make meatballs. Are you hungry, Gavin?"

"I could eat but— "

"It'll be about an hour. Just have to warm up these homemade meatballs. You know, I use Italian sausage and special herbs."

Brianne could almost hear the poor man's stomach growling.

"Mom, we have some reports to file and work to do."

Janet gave her an as-if glance. "You can do that while I cook."

Brianne knew when she'd been beaten. "Okay then."

Her mother stopped everything and came over to give her a hug and kiss. "How are you, baby?"

"I'm good," Brianne said, shooting Gavin an apologetic look over her mother's shoulder. "We've just been so busy with this investigation."

Janet held up a hand. "I know you can't discuss it. And I get that. I'd hoped you'd come out to the beach and visit with us."

"I wanted to, but work."

"Yes, work. So go down and work and I'll call you when it's ready." Then she leaned down. "Hello, Miss Stella. How are you today?"

Stella barked and pranced, knowing a treat might be in her future. Serpico lifted his little head and snarled again.

"You are a good girl," Janet purred to Stella. Then she got busy again, pulling out frozen things and humming to herself. "It's so good to be home. I love my sister, but you know how that goes."

"I'm glad you're home, too, Mom," Brianne said. Then she motioned to Gavin. "We can go down to my apartment. Mom, can I help with dinner?"

"No. Go do your work so we can visit later."

Brianne obeyed her too-interested mother and indicated to Gavin to get moving. They hurried down the stairs, the K-9 following them. Serpico got up and inserted himself into the fun, too, Stella playing with him in a friendly fashion.

When they were downstairs, Brianne turned to Gavin. "I'm so sorry."

He grinned and leaned down to show Serpico he was not the enemy, letting the scared little dog sniff his knuckles. "Why apologize? I'm the one who frightened your poor mother."

Brianne giggled. "As you can see, my *poor* mother can hold her own."

"Good point," he replied. "So...I'm staying for dinner?"

"Yes, you are."

She moved around the kitchen and found them two sodas. "Meantime, make yourself at home and prepare to be interrogated."

"This should be interesting," Gavin replied, his eyes soft on her.

Brianne decided he made this apartment seem so small. He filled it and her life with a definite presence that enveloped her in a tingly, charged awareness.

"Are you okay with this?" he asked, misreading her silence.

"I don't think I had a choice," she replied, meaning

more than just another meal with him. "But you sure seem to be hanging out at my house a lot."

"I know," he said, serious now. "I could get used to this."

"One day, I'd like to see your home, Gavin."

"That can be arranged. But I don't cook much."

"I don't, either, but once you've had my mother's famous spaghetti and meatballs, you won't go hungry again. She'll want to feed you forever."

"That sounds like a fair trade."

She nodded. "Okay, let's get down to work."

He stretched and took his weapon out of his waistband and laid it on a high shelf. "Where do we start?"

His question should have been regarding work, but Brianne sensed he was asking her a personal question.

Where would they start, once they were finished?

They found a lot of interesting information but nothing criminal regarding Liza Collins.

Gavin read off the findings. "Divorced twice. Daughter to a real estate mogul and third marriage to yet another real estate success—Watson Collins. With her older husband, she became a New York socialite and a powerhouse in the real estate world, but her husband suffered a fatal heart attack after his firm was investigated for embezzlement and fraud."

Brianne nodded along with each word. "Not so much as a traffic ticket on her, but I remember the investigation and how Watson Collins almost lost everything. Liza went to the Wharton School of Business, not to mention making millions in record-breaking housing market sales at a very young age. I'm impressed."

"She's still creepy," Gavin said, his gut burning. "Something about her doesn't sit well with me. And then I told you about that plaid hat I saw on the office shelf in that fancy apartment."

"Yes. Why was it there?"

"Why was a similar baseball cap lying on the roof of that building?"

"And the bomber in the park definitely was wearing the same kind of hat." Brianne looked up at Gavin. "Why would the bomber leave a dog at a construction site?"

"He wanted to lure us there to get rid of us, because you saw him up close and we're both searching for him. But we don't know yet if this was our bomber, although the hat indicates that."

Brianne stared at her notes. "Yes, and he later rigged our vehicle to explode at the garage entrance near the fancy open house." She paused, her brow furrowing, her pen tapping. "But, Gavin, he had a good opportunity to harm us when we followed him to the subway. He could have called for help or turned to attack us."

"He's too smart for a full-on confrontation, Bree. I think he was testing us to see if we'd blow our cover."

"Do you think he planted Scrawny at that building site?"

"You know, the tip about the dog could just be coincidence, like someone suggested."

"True but when we got to that building, someone did try to kill us. What if a random person called in the tip—not knowing anyone else was around. Then Plaid Cap followed us and hid until the other person left and then he tried to kill us with the only weapon he could find—that beam."

Serpico came and nudged Gavin's boot. Gavin lifted the little dog and held him in his lap. The munchkin sure liked to be in on the action.

"He could have tossed one of us off that building or trapped us in the elevator while he put an explosive device on our vehicle again. Or better yet, he could have blown up the building with us in it. But he didn't do any of that."

Brianne's eyes widened, the frown and furrow back. "Maybe he got interrupted by whoever else was there? The person who called in the dog tip?"

"If the bomber tracked us there and tried to get to us, but realized someone else was already there, he would have tried to hide or get away."

"And in his hurry to do that, he lost his hat?"

Brianne twisted a strand of hair falling out of her bun. "Or left it to tease us a little more."

Gavin dropped Serpico down and grabbed his cell phone. "I'm going to find out about surveillance on that building and see if the lab has anything for us yet."

Brianne took Serpico and held him tight, whispering sweet things to the scrappy little Chihuahua. She had a way with animals. And she had a way of making Gavin more centered and focused, too.

He called the lab, knowing someone would still be there. That place never shut down. When Ilana answered, Gavin explained what he needed.

"I was about to call you," the tech said. "We ran the prints you gathered, but we couldn't find a clear set on the doors. Too many to distinguish since it's a construction site."

"And the baseball cap we found? Any DNA on that?"

"Nothing significant on DNA, no. Sorry. However, we did find some synthetic fibers."

"From what?"

"Possibly from a wig. We thought we had a couple of good hair fibers but turned out to be synthetic."

Gavin let that settle over him. "So our man could be wearing a wig under the hat?"

"Yes. Which means not much to find on the hat." Gavin

heard her rustling through some papers. "I'll let you know about anything we find on the dog bowls."

"And the evidence from the park bombing?"

"That's gonna take a few days longer, Gavin."

"Thank you," Gavin said. "I'll check with Danielle about the possible surveillance video on the building site where we located the dog."

Ending the call, he glanced over at Brianne. "They found wig hair on the hat."

"Wig hair?" Brianne gave him a surprised stare. "So our bomber is definitely wearing a wig?"

"Yep—someone was wearing the plaid cap over a wig. Makes sense it could be our bomber since he doesn't want to be recognized and he avoids facing cameras straight on. Probably fake eyebrows, too."

"But we can't prove any of this."

"No, and Noah is going to make us turn this over to the detectives next week. We have to find something soon that can match the Fourth of July bomber with the Tick and the Rexx Agency."

Brianne tapped her pen on her notes. "Liza Collins and Justin Sanelli appear to be clean—and I use that word *appear* loosely, since I think Sanelli is sneaky and too suave and she's creepy and as cold as a frozen salmon. But we've seen someone who looks like our bomber with Morticia. And we think he was at the open house." Shrugging, she said, "Maybe she sends several of them out like minions. Who knows?"

"All we need is one—a strong connection if we can prove it."

"Then we need to keep at it," Brianne said. She picked up her cell phone and called her friend Violet, and told her she was sending pictures of a couple real estate brokers to see if they'd visited Griffin's.

"I'll look them over," Violet said. "Other than what we've told you guys, nothing regarding real estate has escalated. We've had a couple of scary moments with other issues lately but this is a new one. I hope you find these people."

Brianne ended the call and waited for Violet to respond to the photos of Justin Sanelli and Liza Collins.

I don't recognize either of them, Violet texted.

Brianne texted back a thank-you.

Gavin watched Brianne work, knowing she wanted to solve this case, same as him. He wanted to warn her again to be careful but he wanted this bomber, too. Someone was playing a game of cat and mouse with them.

"I'm going to contact Justin again and tell him we're getting impatient. Maybe he can make something happen."

"And we'll be there to make something happen, too," she said, her tone low. "Like several arrests."

Gavin nodded. "Bree, I appreciate all your hard work."

"It's my job."

"Yeah, but—"

"Your dad's home, Bree. Dinner!"

They both sat up in their chairs like guilty teenagers. "My mom has a good set of lungs," she said with a laugh, her tone shaky.

Gavin had been about to go personal, so he was glad her mother had stopped him from doing something stupid like sharing his feelings. *Keep it professional.*

So he said, "And I have a good appetite. That smells so wonderful."

"Okay, let's go eat and then we'll get back at it."

Gavin couldn't argue with that. "Let's do some more searching on Morticia. My gut tells me she's up to her false eyelashes in this mess."

"We'll start there," Brianne said as they moved up the

stairs, two four-legged buddies following them. "Meantime, prepare to meet my dad."

Gavin took a deep breath. "Can't wait."

Already in too deep with Brianne, now he was meeting her folks. *Just dinner with a coworker,* he told himself.

But he sure wouldn't mind it becoming more than that. If he survived this dinner and they solved this case, he might have a glimmer of hope about things moving to a new level with Brianne and him. At least that little gatekeeper Serpico liked him.

SEVENTEEN

Monday morning, Brianne headed to the break room and saw Faith pouring herself a cup of coffee to go with the bagel she had already started nibbling.

"Hey there," Faith said, smiling over her shoulder, the coffeepot in her hand. "Want me to pour you a cup of rocket fuel?"

"Please," Brianne said, Stella at her feet. She rubbed her eyes and stifled a yawn.

"Rough weekend?" Faith asked, her dark curls tucked and pinned behind her ears.

"Up late working through some things."

"Alone or with Gavin?"

Brianne did a mock frown. "Who wants to know?"

"Just about everyone who works here," Faith admitted, "but especially Lani and me."

Brianne took the steaming cup of dark coffee and held it with both hands. "We hung out for a while Saturday. Then I went over everything about this case again last night. So many details to piece together even if I'm officially on desk duty."

"That's every case," Faith said. "Are you still working on Jordan's murder case, too?"

"Yes, but…it's hard to figure that one out since we don't have any solid leads. We didn't have much evidence to work with at that building site where we found Scrawny and we're not even sure if the call was related to Jordan's murder or our bomber."

She wouldn't discuss the details past that information.

"Drink up," Faith said, knowing not to push. "Scrawny is going to have to get a new name soon. He is fast becoming a handsome boy. I think he'll do great as a service dog."

"That's good to hear," Brianne said, her mind on the construction site.

"Want half my bagel?" Faith offered.

Brianne shook her head. "No, I ate at home. Just needed some more caffeine."

Faith left, and Brianne sank down on a chair and thought about having Gavin eat dinner with her parents the other night. Her dad hit it off with him immediately. Soon they were into a long discussion on sports. Baseball was her dad's favorite and Gavin spouted off stats and predictions for the World Series that had Ronald Hayes nodding his head and laughing.

Her dad had winked at her, meaning he approved.

Mom had stood behind the kitchen counter like a judge overseeing a courtroom, her smile serene, her gaze moving with laser-like precision from Gavin to Brianne and back.

Brianne knew that mind. Her mother was probably picturing grandchildren. Several of them. Drat. Now she was picturing a cute baby with Gavin's big brown eyes.

"Stop it," Brianne said. As if she could.

"Excuse me?"

Brianne glanced up to find Sophie Walters staring at her.

"Oh, hi, Sophie. Didn't hear you come in." Or she wouldn't have been talking to herself.

"I guess not," Sophie said, her smile as pretty as ever. Her blue eyes missed nothing, though. Brianne liked Sophie and she was happy for Sophie and Luke and all of her other friends who'd found love despite their tough jobs.

That might not work for her, however.

"Sorry, I was talking to myself." She glanced at the box of doughnuts someone had kindly left on the counter. "I want a doughnut, but I have to refrain."

Brianne had been eating way too much lately. Her mom's meatballs were her favorite and she'd had another plateful last night. But she'd especially enjoyed watching Gavin's face on Saturday during his first bite of a meatball with her mom's homemade spaghetti sauce.

He'd looked like a little boy on Christmas.

"Seriously good," he'd said, still chewing.

Her mother had fallen in love with him at that moment.

And maybe, Brianne had, too.

Stop it, she said to herself this time.

But no one heard her thoughts. Except maybe Stella. The astute dog lifted her head and stared at Brianne, hoping for a doughnut but offering feminine appreciation.

"Don't tell," Brianne whispered. "We need to get to work."

Okay, now Sophie was looking at Brianne like she'd lost her mind.

Her radio crackled to life. A robbery in progress at a nearby shopping center. Perpetrator getting away on foot.

A 10-31. Robbery. Commercial.

Dumping the rest of her coffee in the trash, she let Sophie know she was responding, grabbed Stella and took off. Even though Stella was being trained for explosive devices, the patrol officers who arrived on the scene would need backup. They could help search to give Stella more out-in-the-field experience.

Brianne got in her SUV, with Stella in the back, and drove the three blocks over.

When she got to the small shopping strip and skidded to a stop, she saw several of New York's finest already on the scene.

Then she spotted Gavin with Tommy walking the perimeters of the small parking lot. They hadn't talked since Saturday night, not even about work since she hadn't found much else on Liza Collins. If the woman was involved, she'd covered her tracks completely.

"Hey," she said, suddenly shy after the way he'd stood at her door Saturday night and smiled at her like a goofy teenager. She'd smiled right back at him, too. Putting that memory away when he only nodded at her in a curt way, she got down to business. "What's the situation?"

"Two males. One, blond and tall, and the other dark-haired and wearing a yellow shirt." He studied the street and watched Tommy for signs of any alerts. "Took off on foot to the east."

"Why aren't we searching?"

He shrugged and readjusted his cap. "We're on standby. Zach and K-9 Eddie took the lead."

"Drug detection?"

He nodded, staying alert, not looking at her. "The store clerk said they both were high on something. They stole cash, bashed her over the head and ran out when she managed to sound an alarm."

Brianne glanced around. The store's front had been cordoned off with crime scene tape and was closed to the public. Patrol officers, K-9 officers and crime scene techs walked in and out, evidence bags in hand. A woman sat in an open ambulance, a wide piece of white gauze covering her head.

Feeling awkward, Brianne smiled at Gavin. "My parents enjoyed meeting you."

"Yeah, they seem like great folks."

So he didn't want to be goofy this morning. Well, she'd told herself to be professional. But that didn't mean they couldn't be polite. *Forget polite.*

She was about to find out what his problem was when they heard a ruckus around the corner. A dog snarled and barked and a human screamed in fear.

"Looks like Eddie found one of our suspects," Gavin said, taking off so fast to check things out that he left her and Stella both prancing in a circle.

Brianne followed, thinking it was going to be a long day. And why was he acting so strangely?

Gavin tried to keep his mind on providing backup while Zach came out of an abandoned building, a cuffed man stumbling and mumbling in front of him. The tall one. Eddie trotted along, clearly proud of apprehending a dangerous drug addict.

But Zach had things under control and the other assailant had been found cowering behind some shipping crates in a corner of that same building, a wad of cash-register money sticking out of his pocket. Nothing much for Gavin to do here.

And nothing to take his mind off Brianne and how she'd somehow made him feel right at home with her folks. Too at home. He'd never felt this way before, as if he belonged. So he'd decided to step back.

Way back. But he needed a lot of distractions.

This kind of work happened on a daily basis. Sad but true.

The busy morning had cleared his head and now he wanted to move on to the next crazy thing that came across the radio.

But he couldn't stop thinking about this weekend and that night around the dinner table with Brianne, her parents, Stella and that little bundle of hair named Serpico.

They'd laughed and joked with each other, the loud love surrounding them a sharp contrast to the quiet his grandmother often demanded in her gentle but firm way. He didn't resent his upbringing and he loved his grandmother, but he'd missed out on that loud love, that flexible, always-going-with-the-flow kind of family dynamic that he'd felt at Bree's house.

He'd felt that love the minute he'd walked in with her that first time. He wished he'd stayed away. It would be hard to walk away now and go back to the silence of his life.

That ache in his heart had subsided last night and now this morning it had come rushing back with all the swift sharpness of a knife cutting through his soul.

"Are you okay?"

Brianne. She'd want answers and he didn't know how to explain things to her without hurting her.

"I'm fine. Just tired."

"Me, too." She started walking with him toward their SUVs. "Can't find anything on Liza Collins, other than she's ruthless and aggressive on winning real estate deals. A good businesswoman but not a people person."

"I set up another meeting with Justin Sanelli," he said before they could move back into a personal conversation. "Thursday at 3:00 p.m. He said he's found some properties that fit what we're looking for. Are you up for it?"

"I'm ready to finish this," Brianne replied, her tone all business, her gaze holding his in a definite challenge. "Are you ready?"

"Yes," he admitted. "I want to get this solved and over with."

"Want to get rid of me, Sutherland?"

He could be honest in his answer. "Not you, Bree. Just this having to look over our shoulders, trying to chase down a man who has no scruples and the amoral people who pay his salary."

"Then I'd say we're both ready," she replied, her tone softer now.

"By the way, Noah cleared us per our last discussion with him. Let's meet at the safe house again." He turned to leave, thinking this was for the best—this pulling back, going neutral, trying to pretend he didn't want more.

"I'll be there."

He could feel her eyes glaring at him. Telling himself he was a coward in the relationship department, Gavin wanted to turn back but he kept walking.

Yep—a long week.

The week turned out to be a busy one for Brianne.

Once they were back from the robbery call, she and Gavin updated two detectives sent from high up on what they'd been doing and what they'd found so far.

The detectives agreed to let them take the lead and they'd be their eyes and ears on the street, as well as backup.

"I don't want you two out there on your own again," Noah had explained in a tone that indicated they'd better not argue with him. They didn't.

Freddie Alverez, a well-liked detective who'd transferred to Queens two years ago, asked Gavin what he could do to help.

"Find Beanpole," Gavin said. "I'm worried about him. He's not showing up in the usual places and he's not answering the burner phone I gave him a month ago."

"You know how street people are," Freddie replied, his dark eyes piercing and steady, his inky hair spiked and shaggy. "They like to hide sometimes."

"I'm still worried," Gavin replied. "Beanpole is usually predictable."

"I'll do what I can," Freddie promised after taking what

information Gavin could give him on the wayward home-less man. "And I'll be your driver come Thursday."

Noah had insisted Gavin and Brianne have a driver each time they went to meet Sanelli. No argument. No more fancy *borrowed* cars.

Several more routine calls, inlcuding one involving a bomb scare in Times Square that turned out to only be a backpack a teenager had left on the bleachers there. Then a possible bomb threat in a building in Chelsea that had her heart pumping and Gavin and Tommy out the door with Stella and Brianne.

Nothing. They'd found nothing in the five-story apart-ment building near 24th Street and Waterside Park, two blocks from the High Line. But both Gavin and Brianne agreed the call had been odd since the building was full of renters and not scheduled for a sale or demolition.

A prankster or someone toying with them again?

"They could have set that up to flush us out," Gavin said to Brianne and Noah later. "Maybe to do some sur-veillance and identify us as Linus and Alice?"

"We were in full uniform with our hats on," Brianne told Noah. "And no one was around. The entire block was cleared."

"But a nervous bomber has ways around that," Gavin said. "This is another one of those non-coincidence things like the shooting at Griffin's and the report of the dog at that building site. Just too close for comfort."

"Finish this," Noah replied. "These people could be on to you or maybe this was random, not connected to your investigation."

Someone had called in a bomb threat, either way, and it had been their job, along with others in the area who'd answered the call, to check things out. Brianne had to hope that with so many uniforms taking over the area, she and

Gavin hadn't been singled out. They'd worked hard to disguise themselves each time they met with Justin Sanelli.

Now, in plain clothes but a disguise nonetheless, Brianne rode the subway from Queens to Manhattan, headed for the safe house just off Broadway. She'd already put the rinse on her hair again and done her face and eyes in heavy makeup. She had an overnight bag with her regular clothes so she could change and go home on the subway and take a cab from the train hub to her house.

As usual, the afternoon commute was crowded. Brianne had her hair covered with a large floppy hat and she wore big dark sunglasses.

Don't act like a cop, Brianne thought. Stella would be waiting for her with a handler at the safe house—to help protect Brianne while she was there alone. Since regular pets had to be in a carrier to ride the subway, this was the best plan. Usually when they were both suited up in their uniforms, people on the subway made a wide berth. No one wanted to be taken down by a K-9 officer and her four-legged partner. Dog bites hurt. But Stella would guard first, and only bite if ordered.

She missed her K-9 partner. Having Stella with her as much as possible gave the dog training hours and gave Brianne some protection. A precaution Gavin and she had agreed on, at least. But Brianne had her weapon nearby, and she covertly studied the passengers getting on the train.

Nervous about being on assignment with Gavin again today, she watched the crowded car and wondered why he'd pulled away after what she considered a successful meeting with her overly protective parents. Maybe too successful. Or he didn't like having family so involved in his work. Or just her family? Did he want to be a loner the rest of his life? Or did he not want to be with her?

Brianne couldn't figure it out, but she used the hour or so on the train to consider Gavin from every angle. She came to one conclusion.

He was afraid of loving anyone. He'd lost so many people in his life, why would he want to risk everything for her?

I should be worth it.

She wanted to be worthy of someone's love but this life, this job made that hard. Maybe they were too much alike, too determined and ambitious and stubborn to take things beyond work.

Glancing around, Brianne tugged her hat close and watched people at each stop.

Then she noticed a man with dark shaggy hair and heavy eyebrows getting on at the station. He looked a lot like The Plaid Cap man!

Brianne snuggled down in her seat and kept her hat low. If she could get a good look, she could ID him and report this. Or follow him.

Gathering her wits, she watched as he sat down a good distance away, many people between them. As far as she could tell, he hadn't noticed her. But would he spot her when she had to exit? Or should she follow him?

Brianne took a breath and formed a plan. She'd stay on until the man got off the train and then she'd alert Gavin to send one of the detectives to tail Plaid Cap. She couldn't take on this man on her own, as much as she wanted to. She texted Gavin and told him which train she was on and who had joined her.

On it, he texted back. Be careful.

When Plaid Cap stood to exit, Brianne knew she had to do as Gavin asked. This was her exit, too.

EIGHTEEN

Gavin got out of the car he'd brought to take them to meet Justin Sanelli and hurried up to the Gable Hotel's double front doors. Detective Freddie Alvarez sat in the driver's seat, wearing a chauffeur cap and dark clothes. There as backup, he'd make sure no devices were put on the car.

Glad for the help, Gavin hurried to get Brianne, who should be in their room. Noah had put patrols all the subways around Manhattan based on what she'd texted so that Plaid Cap could be tailed, but so far nothing. And he'd heard nothing from Brianne, either.

He went through the front door of the old hotel and nodded to the front desk clerk, also an undercover detective taking over for today only. They'd covered all the bases.

When he knocked on the door of the suite, Gavin steeled himself. Tommy looked up at him with loyal eyes, always ready to do his job.

The door opened, and he took in the sight of Brianne in a flowing floral summer dress and strappy sandals, a small shoulder bag hanging over her arm, the gold designer initial on it winking at him. Just big enough to get a weapon in, he imagined. She wore her hair up in a messy bun and long swaying earrings hung like miniature wind chimes from her ears.

Breathless, she said, "Let's go."

"Are you all right?" he asked, thinking he sounded neutral while his heart was anything but neutral. And she smelled like summer, fresh and clean.

"Fine." Turning to Stella, she ordered the curious Lab to stay and pointed to the doggie bed the hotel had provided for their suite. Their friend downstairs would check on Stella and take her for a walk. "I got here late. I followed Plaid Cap into the crowd but...he slipped out a side door."

"Brianne..."

"Don't fuss, Gavin," she whispered as they headed out. "I had to keep an eye on him until I saw one of our detectives nearby."

"He could have turned and recognized you."

"I was heavily disguised in a huge floppy hat and my sunglasses."

They got into the backseat of the sedan, the detective turned chauffeur at the wheel.

"The building is in Chelsea," Gavin said, deciding he wouldn't chastise her, but later he'd have to discuss this with her. "Three blocks from where the bomb threat happened earlier this week."

"Hmm, that's interesting," Brianne added, keeping her voice low. "I think the Tick sent us a calling card." Then she sat up. "What if he's going to the same place?"

"We'll know soon," Gavin replied, his expression going dark. "If they're playing us, I'd rather meet them head-on than let them walk."

"I don't want these people doing their dirty work anymore."

"We can agree on that," he replied, his gut churning.

"So what's the building?"

"The CHL—Chelsea-Highline, but Justin called it the CHL Condos. He says the building is *vulnerable* and needs a lot of work. But the seller's asking price is high."

"So a perfect building for him to mess with," Brianne said, her gaze moving over the traffic.

His phone buzzed. Gavin answered and then thanked the detective on the line. Turning to Brianne, he said, "Plaid Cap got away again. Turned into an alley and managed to disappear."

"I hate not knowing where he is and what he's doing."

"Ditto. But we have strong backup and we have to play our parts."

Freddie pulled the sleek black car up to the redbrick building that shot toward the sky.

"This one really does look like a bargain," Gavin said before they got out. "Maybe fifteen floors."

Brianne stared up at it, her eyes dark. She'd gone off on her own today—following Plaid Cap until she'd spotted a cop on his trail. What if she hadn't seen their backup? How could he get past that?

Work. Focus on work.

"I'll be around the corner," Freddie said with a final nod.

They both had tiny wireless mic pieces hidden in their clothing. Bree's was in the neckline of her dress, and Gavin's was taped onto the handkerchief in his lapel in case they needed to warn the two detectives assigned to watch out for them.

Gavin guided Brianne and Tommy into the small lobby, noticing the exits down hallways each way and the two elevator bays behind the unmanned reception desk. No doorman and not much security. Justin waited next to the mailboxes near the elevators.

"Hello, you two," Justin said, all sweetness and light, his dark shades hooked on the pocket of his white button-up shirt. He air-kissed Brianne and gave Gavin a quick, firm handshake. "I think I've found the perfect place for you."

"It's drab," Brianne said, doing a sweep over her pulled-down sunshades. "But I can see the potential."

Justin nodded, his icy blue eyes twinkling. "I believe you know how to overcome drab, Mrs. Reinhart."

"Linus, what do you think?" he asked, shifting his weight from one Italian loafer to the other before tentatively reaching out to pet Tommy. The spaniel allowed it, his head up while Justin scratched between his ears.

So Tommy didn't think Justin was a bad guy—or at least had no scent related to making bombs. The man did like his aftershave, however.

Gavin watched as Brianne steered Tommy back by her side and then gave the place his full attention. "I think I should be able to get the best possible price—a low bid. This place needs some serious tender loving care."

"Good, good," Justin said, beaming. "Let's take the full tour."

He took them past the shabby unmanned desk, explaining that most of the former tenants had moved out and the building was slowly becoming empty. The owner wanted to sell, but he was being stubborn about the price and refused to negotiate.

"But I have one ace left in the hole," the bubbly broker said as he hit the tarnished elevator buttons.

Gavin's gaze met Brianne's. They both knew what that ace might be. This investigation was about to move forward.

Finally.

Once he had the Tick behind bars, Gavin had big plans of his own. He planned to find a way to overcome the solid wall of fear he had each time he thought about being with Brianne.

There had to be a way to crack that wall, same as cracking a major case. He hoped. He prayed.

* * *

Brianne held Tommy's leash tightly when they exited on the fifteenth floor. The penthouse.

"This whole floor could be your apartment," Justin explained. "It's four different apartments with hallways running between them in a four-square design. Tear out three of the kitchens and knock out a couple of walls and you'd have close to six-thousand square feet, several large bed and baths and a view of different areas of the city from every room."

Brianne could hear the gleeful greed in his words. "Yes, this could work," she said, smiling to hide the anger whirling through her. "Or we could just tear down the building and start over." Spotting the Hudson River, she added, "I'd kill for this view."

Justin gasped and put a hand to his mouth. "We won't have to go quite that far for you to get it."

Brianne smiled knowingly at Gavin, not even having to pretend. "I would hope not."

Justin moved them through the main apartment, pointing out the pros and cons. "There's the High Line. It's just around the block. You can stroll to your heart's desire. Tommy here would love that, right?"

Tommy woofed right on cue.

They all laughed. "I think he agrees," Gavin said.

"And you have dining on one of the piers by the river at sunset—just two blocks to the west. And, of course, Chelsea Market on Ninth Avenue, again with the High Line passing through on Tenth Avenue."

"You're reeling me in, Justin," Brianne said, her hand on Justin's buff arm. "Keep talking."

He showed them another apartment on the other side, smaller, but with more panoramic views. "There's the Empire State Building."

"Amazing," Gavin said, his tone just below giddy.

"Not to mention the Flower Market and Chelsea Park," Justin added. "This place is going to shine. It has everything nearby you'd ever need." Then he did a mock-pout. "But *it* needs someone to give it the attention required to turn it into a gleaming modern apartment building. Who says gentrification isn't a good thing?"

"Not me," Brianne replied, wanting to strangle him. "But brand-new is always good, too."

They finished viewing the entire top floor and came back to the biggest of the four apartments.

"Impressive," Gavin said. "What do you think, Alice in Wonderland?"

Brianne chuckled. "Darling, I think I'm *in* Wonderland."

"Justin, I think we have a winner," Gavin said to the eager man standing there with them.

"I do, too," Brianne said, her arms opening wide. "I can see it now. A huge gourmet kitchen here, open to the fabulous den and living area. We'll add more windows and glass doors so I won't miss out on any part of this incredible view. And the bedrooms… What, maybe four or five, at least? And the baths. We'll redo all of them and add bigger closets, of course."

"I hear the swish of my money leaving my hands," Gavin said with a laugh.

"So do I," Justin chimed in. "I hope a large chunk of it lands in my hands."

Gavin pulled Brianne close. "Is this the one?"

"Let's look at the entire building," she replied. "We'll have to bring in people, inspectors, surveyors, the works, but this building has good bones. I think we should make an offer."

"Strong bones," Justin quipped, sensing a deal. "I'm guessing it can withstand anything."

Gavin kissed Brianne. "I'm thinking that same thing." Then he told Justin their low-end price, a sum that boggled Brianne's mind but made the greedy broker wince.

But the kiss had boggled her mind *and* her heart. It was quick, efficient and…wonderful. What would a real kiss from Gavin do to her?

How would they ever pull this off? And how would she ever get over her feelings for him?

Later at Griffin's, Gavin sat down with Brianne inside the Dog House, the room reserved for NYPD's best. They were both exhausted, starving and glad they'd made the next move with Sanelli. No sign of Plaid Cap, however. Why did the man keep slipping away?

"So everything is in place since I filled out paperwork on this months ago and got clearance to make an offer within a certain amount. We can deliver the down payment by Tuesday," Gavin said once they'd ordered their meals. "They will never cash the check, however."

They'd left Justin Sanelli a very happy man. Now they both decided on Barb's baked chicken and rice with string beans on the side. A good hearty meal.

"That's a lot of zeroes," Brianne said after sipping her iced tea. "But Sanelli won't get his hands on any of the department's cash."

"Not with us to stop it."

They sat talking for a few minutes, Tommy and Stella lying at their feet. The place wasn't too busy tonight. Only a cluster of other officers in plain clothes in a corner and several tables of loud patrons in the main area.

"You charmed Sanelli," Gavin said, thinking she'd already charmed him. She had a good laugh and a great smile. He'd given her a spontaneous kiss while pretending.

He wondered what it would be like to kiss her in the quiet when they were alone and off duty.

But would they ever reach that point?

He was working two undercover operations here—the bomber case and the case of slowly falling for a woman he couldn't have. How long could he keep pretending?

The kitchen door next to their table swung open. The waiter bringing their food stopped, his body holding the door while one of the chefs asked him about an order. The scents and sounds from the kitchen wafted through the room.

Tommy and Stella both stood, lifted their heads and stared at the kitchen door.

Gavin sent Brianne a glance. "Time to move."

"Get out of the doorway," Gavin said to the surprised waiter.

The young man stepped out into the restaurant and then set their food, tray and all, on the table. "What's wrong?"

The chef stood inside the door, holding it. "Hey, officers, what's up?"

The other officers immediately stood, too.

Brianne motioned them to the door. "We got an alert from our partners." Turning to the chef, she said, "Get Lou and everyone out of the kitchen. We need to search it now."

The off duty officers knew what to do.

"I'll call it in," one of them said.

"I'll clear the main room," another one called, heading toward the closed glass door between this room and the other dining area. His voice boomed, "NYPD. People, clear the room. Get out now!"

Gavin and Brianne hurried through the swinging door. "We need to search the kitchen," Gavin called, seeing Louis coming toward him. "Lou, stop everything and get everyone out of here."

Lou didn't asked questions. "Turn off the stoves and burners and get out," he ordered.

Two other officers arrived and shouted, "Let's go. Now!"

His staff did as he told them, knowing when two K-9 officers came into their workspace that something was up.

"Search. Find."

Tommy and Stella trotted around the long square kitchen, their snouts moving from ground to air. When Tommy alerted on one of the storage rooms, Gavin knew they were in for trouble. Stella immediately did the same, sniffing, sitting and then looking back at them.

"Come," Gavin and Brianne ordered, getting the dogs away as quickly as possible.

They rushed out the side doors and hurried onto the street, sirens wailing in the distance and patrol cars skidding to a stop down the street.

"Everyone out?" Gavin called.

"Yeah," Lou called back, holding Barb by his side. Their daughter, Violet, stood with them, her eyes wide and her hand to her mouth.

Gavin hurried Brianne and the dogs out to the cordoned-off street. Before he could turn to look back, Griffin's Diner exploded.

NINETEEN

Brianne's ears rang with all the force of a thousand crickets chirping against her skull. She lay flat, waiting, the acrid smell of something burning bringing her out of her fog.

"Bree?"

She lifted and felt two strong hands pulling her around.

Gavin. He had another gash, this one on the left side of his jaw. The man would be scarred for life if they didn't end this. Soot rained down on them, but he sat back on the concrete and held her close with a hand on each arm. His eyes and his expression full of shock and worry.

"Are you all right?" he asked, his words echoing as if from far away.

She nodded and pointed to her ears.

"Me, too," he said, shaking his head.

Paramedics came running and pointing the ambulance. "Here, let's get you to a bus."

"I'm fine." She managed to stand on wobbly legs, then held out her hand to help Gavin up. Tommy and Stella stood a few feet away, watching and waiting.

Once they were standing, the action around them came to her full-blown and chaotic. "Gavin," she whispered. "I'm so sorry this happened." Touching at her head, she whispered, "I shouldn't have let him out of my sight earlier today."

"This is not your fault," he replied, his hand pushing at her messy hair. "Are you sure you're okay?"

"Just another bruise to add to my collection." She touched a hand to his cut. "You're bleeding."

"I'll be fine. Let's get to it."

They turned to see the damage. A hole gaped in the roof, fire shooting up out of it. The fire department hosed it down in minutes, but the building had suffered damage.

"The kitchen is toast," Lou said when they went to find him. "Pun intended." He held his hands up in the air and then dropped them down. "I don't know if we can come back from this."

Barbara wiped at her eyes. "We always come back, Louis Griffin. Don't let them run us out."

"No one is going to run you out," Brianne said, her ears still full of what felt like cotton, her head throbbing.

"We'll find whoever did this. In the meantime, you two get checked and make sure your employees and customers are safe."

Barbara shot her a thankful smile. "She's right, Lou. Let's see how your blood pressure is holding up."

No loss of lives, but the place would be closed until they could rebuild.

Violet stood by, tears in her eyes. "Zach is on his way," she said, reaching for her mother and falling into Barbara's arms.

"Everyone got out alive," Barbara said. "If Bree and Gavin hadn't been here with their partners, we might not have survived."

Gavin breathed in a long breath. "I'm going to talk to the fire chief."

Brianne sense he wanted to do that alone, so she called for Stella. "I'll do a search for shrapnel and maybe find something to help us."

"No, you need to be checked over first," Violet insisted. "Some people are being sent to the hospital. Let one of the paramedics make sure you're okay."

"Later," Brianne said. "Right now, it's important to find evidence before this place gets contaminated even more."

"Bree," Violet said, stopping her with a hand on her arm. "Do you think this was aimed at my parents?"

Brianne couldn't lie. "We don't know yet, but yes, we think so." She couldn't tell her friend this might be because of Gavin and her. They didn't know yet and she needed to keep the details hushed to protect all of them.

But she knew in her heart, this had been deliberate.

Brianne took Stella to walk the perimeters of the block, ignoring reporters and people gawking. She was searching for something and someone. But she didn't see anyone who matched their bomber in the crowd. He'd probably detonated the explosive from a cell phone. She'd let him slip away.

Turning back, she told herself she wouldn't stop until she found the person who'd done this.

Once she'd finished, Brianne found Gavin and they let the dogs do another sweep inside the building, keeping busy while the bomb squad finished investigating.

Tommy stopped again near where the storage room had once been. Now only a few beams of the wall around that area remained. The wood, drywall and the supplies stored there had all been blown into jagged pieces and tiny particles.

"What is it?" Gavin asked. "Find."

Tommy sniffed and lowered his snout, staying close in a corner. "He's got something."

Brianne turned to a patrolman standing nearby. "Hey, send someone from the bomb squad over here."

Gavin took a still-smoking fragment of lumber and carefully shifted through the pile of rubble at the dog's feet. When he saw a rectangle black box with wires twisting away from it, he patted Tommy on his head. "Good dog. Good find, Tommy."

"What is it?" Brianne asked from behind.

"I think Tommy found the detonator," he replied.

A member of the bomb squad came over and looked at the device. "I'd say this did the deed, Gavin. Let's get it to the lab pronto."

Gavin nodded. "It could match the one we found on the Fourth of July bombing site in East River Park."

After the bomb tech left, he turned to Brianne. "This might be our break." Staring at the corner where they'd found the device, he added, "I think the Tick just made a big mistake."

This latest explosion had shifted things into full speed ahead. From the commissioner on down, Gavin and Brianne's undercover work now had the approval of the whole department, the FBI and any other agency that had an interest in this investigation.

"You'll finish it with our full backing," Noah told them two days later. "The money is in place for the down payment. Don't hand over that check until the last minute. We need concrete proof of what these corrupt individuals have been doing for years now." Then he added, "I had to call in some favors with a couple of friends in the FBI to keep them from taking over this case. They'll be watching, and they expect a full report on your activities. Do your best and come out of this alive, okay?"

"Yes, sir," they both said.

Gavin and Brianne left Noah's office and quickly walked toward the training arena.

Gavin took her by the arm and tugged her into an empty office. "Bree, before we finish this, I need to talk to you."

"What's the matter?" she asked, those incredible eyes drenching him with a heart-wrenching longing.

He wanted to tell her what he'd realized yesterday—

that life was too short to fight against what your heart was shouting to you. But it sounded cliché in his mind. And he wasn't good with words.

Maybe if he just showed her.

"I just wanted to—" His phone buzzed. Groaning, he said, "Don't go anywhere."

"Okay." She stood still and waited, her pretty face frowning.

"Hey, Ilana," he said. Then he listened. "We'll be right there."

He hung up and took Brianne by the hand. "They've found something on the Fourth of July bomber. Ilana says they've got something that indicates matches to the Williamsburg bomb and the one at Lou's two days ago."

She followed him but pulled back. "Gavin, what did you want to tell me?"

Gavin stopped and took a breath, his gut moving ahead of his logic. Tugging her close, he kissed her on the lips, not caring right now who might see them.

When he pulled away, he was rewarded with a stunned gaze and what looked like the same longing that churned inside of him. "Just that," he said. "Just in case."

"In case of what?" she asked, breathless.

"In case this thing goes bad," he replied.

Then he hurried her back out to their vehicles. "Maybe the lab found something we can use to end this."

Brianne gave him another stunned glance. "Then we should pray that this case won't go bad."

That comment gave Gavin hope that she'd liked kissing him.

But before he could explore that theory closer, they had a lot of work to do.

* * *

"So you see these little wires right here?" Ilana asked, her magnifying glass in her hand.

Gavin squinted and pointed. "Yes. Did those wires cause the explosion?"

"Partly," Ilana explained, her brow furrowed. "You know that bombers have a signature. Sometimes it's easy to find, sometimes impossible. This one is really good at hiding his work, but ego gets them every time. He left us a distinguished design and it's all there in these little wires."

Brianne took the magnifying glass. "What are we looking at?"

Ilana beamed and held her hands together. "So bomb-makers have a tendency to do special curls and twists in the wiring when they're creating an explosive device." She moved to her microscope. "The device you're seeing has an interesting wire twist."

She pointed to the microscope standing on a nearby table. "Gavin, look at this."

Gavin leaned down and looked through the microscope. "Is this the same device?"

"Nope," Ilana said on a proud note. "It's the one the techs found at the Fourth of July bombing."

Gavin stood and let Brianne look into the microscope while he studied the other device through the magnifying glass. "And this one came from Griffin's, right?"

"You are correct," Ilana said, pushing at her dark glasses. "They match almost completely. So I was curious and I went back to the device you and Tommy found at the Williamsburg explosion."

"But that scene didn't show anything definitive," he reminded her. "The fire department decided what we'd found was part of the boiler panel."

"Or so we thought," Ilana replied, moving to a table

where she had pictures of both the scene and the fragments laid out.

Pointing to a particular photo, she said, "We found some wiring, but the tech thought it came from the boiler's system—the breaker box."

"And you're saying it didn't?" Gavin asked.

"Yes, I'm saying that," Ilana replied. "I think your bomber is left-handed, Gavin. Whoever it is, they like swirls in their wires. Very intricate, dainty swirls."

Brianne's gaze hit Gavin. "So we've got a match on the same bomber for all three locations?"

"Yes, we do," Ilana replied. "And…I saved the best for last. We also found some epidermis on this last device. Just enough to compare to the touch DNA we found from the Fourth of July bombing."

"Did you get a match?"

"William Caston, aka the Tick, is your bomber, Gavin. At all three sites."

Gavin couldn't speak. He nodded and stared down at the evidence. "Now we have to find him."

"Well, when you do, you'll have some interesting comparisons to show him," the proud tech said with a grin.

"Thank you," Brianne said, giving Ilana a little hug.

They left the lab, quiet until they were outside alone. "This is huge," Gavin finally said. "We need to report this to Chief Jameson."

"I agree," Brianne said. "We need to set up our final meeting with Justin Sanelli. We have proof that the bomber was at all three sites. Now we need to find the person who hired him to do this."

"And set up a sting to finally bring the Tick to justice," Gavin added.

Gavin's phone rang before they made it back to the department's main floor.

"Sutherland," he said.

"Gavin, this is Freddie Alverez. Listen, I have news on your CI."

Gavin motioned to Brianne to wait. "You found Beanpole?"

"Yeah, but Gavin, it's not good. We found his body in some bushes near Battery Park. I'm sorry, but looks like he's been dead for a week or so, according to the ME."

Gavin hung his head. "He had a favorite spot near Battery Park. Do you know what happened?"

"Blunt force trauma. He has a deep wound in the back of his head. The ME said he probably went with the first blow."

Gavin closed his eyes. "Thank you, Freddie. I'll want to see the report and the body."

"Understood," Freddie replied. "Got to go."

Gavin hung up and stared over at Brianne. "Beanpole is dead. Blunt force trauma. I have to go and see him and get the details."

She grabbed his arm. "Oh, Gavin, I'm so sorry. Someone killed him?"

"It looks that way," he said, his heart sick. "And I think we both know who that someone was."

TWENTY

A day later, Gavin stood with Brianne in the Gable Hotel suite. "Ready?"

She smiled up at him, her hair caught up in a twirl on her head, the dark strands almost as much a part of her as her brilliant red tresses. But he liked the red best.

"As ready as ever," she said, the smile going to steel. "I want to end this."

He looked her over, enjoying this pretending but anxious to get on with the real deal—her. She wore a sleeveless olive green high-necked sweater and a full black long skirt over shimmering gold-burnished heeled sandals.

"You know," he began, "I've never noticed fashion much before, but you sure know how to pull off these designer looks."

She laughed and patted her hair, her gold hoop earrings winking at him. "I'll miss these fancy clothes but I like my jeans and T-shirts just as much as this overpriced getup."

"You look good in any outfit, Bree," he said, taking her hands in his. "And before we get wired for our own protection, I just wanted to continue our discussion from the other day."

"Which discussion?"

He grabbed her close and leaned down to kiss her. "This one."

Gavin placed his hands in her hair and pulled her close, loving the way she sighed and fell into the kiss. Did she feel the same way? Did she want this to keep going?

They parted, and he looked down at her, the feel of her soft curls warm against his hands. "Bree, I don't want anything to happen to you."

"Nothing is going to happen to me," she said. "Except my hair is now messed up."

He held his hands in place. "You look liked you've just been kissed."

"Oh, part of the cover?"

"No. A real kiss." Then he dropped his hands and stepped back. "I guess it's silly, but I never knew what happened to my mother. If she's dead or alive or if she ever thought about what she'd done. That unresolved uncertainty makes me cautious and too protective."

Brianne's gaze filled with understanding. "Did you do this with Granny Irene? Did you watch out for her?"

"I tried but she had a large dose of pride. She thought she needed to be the one taking care of me."

"Well, Sutherland, she did a fine job on that and I'm thinking you did, too."

"So you get it?"

"I get it. I'm touched and amazed and… I like this discussion. But we've got business to take care of."

She seemed to be shutting him down. But she turned back before he could say anything else. Grabbing him by his white button-up shirt, she leaned up. "You take care, too. You're not the only one who's protective around here."

Gavin nodded, unable to say anything more.

Then he said a silent prayer for their protection and thanked God for partnering him with a woman who could not only match him but outshine him, too.

"Okay, Brianne, let's get this done. This should be our last meeting with Justin Sanelli."

"I sure hope so," Brianne replied.

Freddie knocked and came in to wire them. "So we can

keep track of you two and communicate," he explained. "But anything you do or say will be heard, so keep that in mind."

No more personal talk. Gavin thought, smiling at Brianne.

Soon they were on their way out the door. On the ride over, Brianne tried to absorb that kiss. This one had been deep and meaningful and full of a sweet warmth that left her longing for more. But would they get a chance to explore these feelings without the guise of pretending?

Freddie watched them settling into the dark sedan and turned to man the wheel. "We'll be in Chelsea in about twenty minutes since we're early for rush hour. Rest up and get your heads in the game."

Gavin sat quiet with Tommy tucked against his jeans wearing a leather collar with some hardware on it to give it a moto edge.

The dog had been a trouper, doing what he needed to do and staying out of the way unless told otherwise. Stella would be with them when they took in the Tick. If that happened according to plan.

As they entered the Rexx Agency offices, she smiled, but inside her nerves dinged and banged against her system, giving her a buzz that was part adrenaline and part anticipation. She would be careful.

Because she had a good reason to fight to the finish on this one. It had taken a lot for Gavin to confess his worst fears to her earlier. He had a scar on his heart that needed to be healed. She wanted to be the one to help with that.

Freddie pulled the car up to the lobby of the modern steel-and-chrome building. "This is it, my friends. Remember the code word for help: 'no deal.'"

"I'm planning on getting the deal," Gavin replied.

The dark shining in his eyes reminded Brianne of the building they were about to enter.

Unyielding.

"So this is it." Justin Sanelli looked like he might pass out from pure greed. "Soon, your name will be on the CHL building."

"It's happening," Brianne said with the same greedy glee. "I can't wait to put our stamp on it."

Justin's glee went south. "The seller tentatively agreed to your price, but the paperwork hasn't arrived yet."

Gavin gave the man an intimidating glare. "Make it happen, Justin."

Looking nervous, Justin made a call. "Speed things up. My clients are tired of playing games."

He listened for a moment and then ended the call and turned back. "I hate to tell you this but…one of the tenants is waffling. He's threatening the building owner with a boycott or something. The seller is getting cold feet since this tenant is standing in the way of the deal.

"What?" Gavin asked, real frustration clear in his words. "We agreed on this, Justin. We're about to hand you a very big down payment and sign the rest of the papers."

Sanelli shrugged. "The hold-out is a tough old bird."

"Obviously." Brianne went into full Alice-mode. "This won't do. I thought we had a deal."

"And we still have a deal," Sanelli said. "I told you I will make it happen. Give me twenty-four hours to talk both the seller and the tenant into this."

"I don't know." Gavin stood, pacing and shot Justin a rage-fueled stare. "You'd better come up with something, Sanelli."

Justin stood, too. "I'll be right back."

He left the room with an abrupt swish.

Gavin kept up the facade. "Don't worry, honey. We can offer more money. You know I'll do whatever it takes."

The door opened, and Justin came in with Liza Collins.

"I'm so sorry," she said, her dark hair held to one side with a wide clip that allowed it to cascade over her shoulder, the scent of something spicy lingering around her. Wearing a crisp white blouse and cream linen pants, she held up a white sheet of paper with something typed on it. Sitting down, she signed the paper with an elegant burgundy pen, her jewels flashing. "The building is nearly empty, but there's always someone who wants to make a last stand. This is my signature. My word that we will make this right—a good faith document that I rarely give out. If we don't please you, we'll find something else for you within the week."

Gavin took the paper and stared down at the swirls in her signature. "I'll hold you to that." Handing the paper to Brianne, he asked, "What do you want to do, darling?"

Brianne stared at the paper, her eyes going wide. "I think we should give the Rexx Agency one final opportunity to give us what we're asking for." Then she glanced across the table at Liza. "Twenty-four hours or we walk."

The other woman's expression filled with rigid surprise, but something dark and daring passed through her eyes.

They left, not having to pretend disappointment and anger.

"We'll surveil the building in question," Gavin told Freddie when they were back in the car. "If the bomber compromises the building, the seller and the unhappy tenant should both be ready to make a deal."

"Already called it in," Freddie replied. "This is where we take over. We'll convince the tenant to get out—a gas leak or pest control excuse—and make sure the building is empty."

"When the Tick is inside doing the deed, Bree and I want to take him," Gavin said.

Freddie nodded. Gavin told Brianne he'd be watching the monitors for the next twenty-four hours. "The bomber is going to make a move. I'm pretty sure the person Sanelli contacted is giving the orders. They're not only sabotaging buildings but also gouging clients."

"I'll watch with you," she replied. "I won't be able to sleep, anyway."

Gavin nodded, his face washed in shadows, his eyes rimmed with fatigue. He tugged her close but stayed silent.

They went back to the safe house and then waited until dark to leave separately in unmarked cars driven by fellow officers.

Once they were at headquarters, they headed into the tech department and took seats behind the IT experts who'd sent out two other detectives to monitor the building.

Brianne came in with coffee and sat with Gavin. "Hey, I noticed something interesting about Liza Collins today."

"Okay, what?"

"She's left-handed," Brianne said, her gaze meeting his.

Gavin let that sink in, remembering the swirls in her penmanship. "Swirls," he said. "Swirls and twists."

Brianne nodded. "Just like the wires used to set off these bombs."

"Left-handed and has a thing for making swirls."

"That can't be coincidence," Brianne whispered. "Do you think we've been after the wrong person all along?"

Gavin let out a breath. "It all makes sense now, doesn't it?"

"The bomber didn't show."

Gavin hated saying the words, but he and Brianne had spent a long night piecing this investigation together.

"Is he onto you?" Noah asked, while the other team members sat listening.

"We don't know," Gavin admitted. "But we're not giving up yet." Looking over his notes, he added, "We've learned a few things."

"Such as?"

"We think there were two people on that roof when the beam came down the other day."

Brianne added her thoughts. "We think someone deliberately brought the dog there and reported it, but meantime the Tick could have been at the building already and had to hide from the other person."

Noah mulled that over. "So this other person knows something about Jordan's murder and was messing with the department by bringing a German shepherd-mix there?"

"Yes, and they didn't care which of us showed up. The bomber might have been watching Gavin and me, followed us and had to hide once he realized someone else was already there."

"So we still don't know who pushed that beam off the building?" Noah asked. "It could have been either person."

Gavin glanced around the room. "Not sure, and we didn't get any good prints off of the dog bowls or the stair doors."

Brianne leaned in. "We do believe someone wanted us dead. Maybe to distract the unit from Jordan's death, or maybe the bomber wanted to take out Gavin since Gavin and Tommy found what they believed to be the remains of one of his bombs after that explosion in Williamsburg."

"Oh, and one other thing," Gavin added. "We don't have proof yet, but the Tick could be a woman."

Noah let out a grunt. "What?"

Gavin's phone buzzed. "It's Freddie, sir. He's still watching the CHL building."

"What's happening?"

"We've got action. One person entering the building through a back door. Dressed in black, shaggy hair, plaid hat. Building cleared and empty."

"We're on our way," Gavin said. Turning to Noah, he explained, "They only have a couple of hours left before we check in. So they'll blow part of the building today and halt the deal to get a better price."

"Then you need to stop them," Noah said. "Go."

Gavin and Brianne grabbed their gear and hurried to the kennels to suit up Tommy and Stella. "This is the real deal, boys and girls," Gavin said to the dogs after their official protective vests were on.

The two animals stood at attention, ready to do what they'd been trained to do. When the vests went on, the real work began.

"This is it," Brianne said as they rushed out and got into Gavin's vehicle. "This has to be the end of it, Gavin."

"One way or another, it will be," he promised. "Man or woman, we're taking down this person today."

TWENTY-ONE

"All systems go."

The command came over the radio loud and clear, but the plan had changed. Justin had called an hour ago, asking to meet them at the building to give them the good news. The stubborn tenant had caved, and the seller would accept their offer.

"It has to be a setup," Gavin said to Brianne. "Either the seller strong-armed the tenant or they have other plans."

"But we need to go, this time with backup."

She wasn't about to let these people slip away again.

So they got dressed in street clothes and decided they'd take both Tommy and Stella with them, minus their official vests. Carter and Luke and their dogs, Frosty and Bruno, two of the best in their unit, would serve as backup along with the other detectives monitoring the whole thing in an unmarked construction van.

Add to that several uniformed police officers parked nearby and a bomb squad on alert and they were ready to get going. If this was a setup, they'd act as bait and the team would move in and take over.

"If something goes wrong," Gavin said as they strolled toward the CHL building, "promise me you'll take Stella and run."

Brianne did an eye roll. "I promise you I'll draw my weapon and do as I've been trained as a cop and a K-9 officer."

"I don't like that promise."

"What would you do?" she countered, knowing he'd take these people head-on.

"Good point," he replied.

"So we're ready?"

He nodded. "Stella is our new dog. You needed more than one to comfort you and keep you company."

"What if they know we were at the park that day?"

"Yellow Labs are very popular. Stella won't stand out. But it doesn't matter now."

Nothing mattered now, except that she'd fallen in love with him and she wanted to keep him safe. But he might not ever know that.

They entered the building and looked around, "Since we're the 'buyers,' we have good chance of surviving this," Gavin quipped. He stared at his watch and checked the elevators and the desk. "I don't see Sanelli."

Then they heard footsteps. Clicking footsteps.

Liza Collins came toward them, dressed in a bright red tunic over white pants. She wore red leather flat sandals.

A chill went down Brianne's spine, but she shook it off. Both dogs stood at attention, a sure sign that they recognized something in her nearness.

"You have two animals now, I see," Liza said with a sly smile. "You must be dog lovers."

Tommy turned his head, sniffed, glanced back at them.

"Stay, boy," Gavin commanded. "He gets nervous around people sometimes."

"We love animals," Brianne replied, her voice calm, her gaze holding the other woman's. "Dogs make me feel safe. They both need more training so ignore their jitters. It's so nice of you to come here and take care of this, Liza."

Liza motioned for them to follow her. "Oh, I sometimes have to clean up messes and this has turned into a big one."

Gavin chuckled. "Nothing we can't fix, correct?"

"Absolutely," the woman said, her laughter like sharp needles hitting against Brianne's skin. "Let's go into my temporary office, shall we?"

"Where's Justin?" Brianne asked, mainly to alert the team that Liza was alone.

"He's indisposed," Liza replied with a shrug, her creepy laughter echoing around them in a pleased cackle.

She took them to a small room in the lobby that wasn't much bigger than a closet. "Have a seat."

They sat in two folding chairs in front of an old desk. A storage armoire stood in the corner. Tommy again gave Gavin a look. Gavin held the dog's leash tight.

"Did the seller change his mind?" Gavin asked.

"He will before the day is over," Liza said. She didn't sit. Instead, she paced around.

Gavin shook his head. "We came here for a deal. If you don't have one, we're leaving."

Her back to them, Liza stared out the one dingy window that offered a crack of light in this sad little room.

"You won't be leaving at all, Mr. *Reinhart*," she said, whirling to face them.

Then the door slammed behind them.

They turned to see a dark-haired man with bushy eyebrows grinning at them. The Plaid Cap man—minus the hat—held a nasty looking handgun at their backs.

"What's going on?" Brianne said, while the two dogs grew restless. "You're upsetting my babies."

"Cut the act," Liza said. "I've been on to you two for weeks now."

"What do you mean?" Gavin asked, indignation in his words. Then he glanced back. "Who is he and why is he holding a gun on us? What's the matter with you?"

Liza leaned over the desk. "What's the matter with *me*? I'll tell you. You've been lurking about, pretending to be who you aren't, asking a lot of pointed questions. And I want to know why."

Brianne shot Gavin a quick glance. "You already know who we are. You're stalling."

"You won't scam me," Liza said, her voice shaking with anger. "Justin wouldn't confess but I think he's been working with you two to undermine my whole company."

"Excuse me?" Brianne asked. "So you brought us here because you think we're scam artists?"

"No. But your whole marriage and real estate thing is a scam. I saw the way you acted at the open house so I looked you up. Quite impressive. You claim you've come to New York to take over my business. But then, I also spotted you at the park with this Lab. So I did even more research."

Brianne realized the woman either believed they were trying to scam her or had figured out they were cops. So she played along. "What did Justin tell you?"

"He wouldn't talk. But he's been acting strange lately. I have ways of taking care of people who betray me."

"Why would we betray you?" Gavin asked. "We only met you a week or so ago. We just want to find a building to renovate." Laughing, he said, "This is New York. Plenty to go around."

"Not in this market," Liza said with a frown. "Not for you. You followed Bill after the open house. He told me."

"Bill?" Gavin asked, pretending confusion. Then he looked at the silent man behind him.

"My brother," Liza replied. "My twin brother who suffered a head trauma years ago. He does odd jobs for me, hangs around to protect me and occasionally takes care of things."

"Things such as?" Gavin asked.

"See, you're trying to get information out of me. Bill helped me figure this out."

Gavin shrugged. "How do you know you can trust *Bill*?"

Liza hit a hand on the desk. "He's my brother. He wouldn't betray me. I take care of him since his injury left him lacking. Justin was a scaredy-cat, always nervous and wanting to do things by the book. But Bill does anything I ask him to do. It's been that way all of our lives, even after I went through two divorces and an ugly scandal since my last husband died. Justin won't be a problem anymore. You're dealing with me now."

Brianne felt sick to her stomach. Justin Sanelli was probably dead. And this woman was quite mad.

Gavin studied Liza with a cold glare. "It's obvious you have a problem with us, Liza. Justin promised us we'd get this property so we'd like to talk to him."

"I knew it," Liza said, hitting the metal desk so hard she snapped a lacquered fingernail and caused both dogs to twist and bark. "I knew he was double-crossing me."

"How so?" Brianne asked, calming Stella with a soft command.

"Never mind," Liza replied. "Now that I know the truth, I have to go. You've both been interesting, but let's cut to the chase. You're not into real estate. You're cops and not very good ones since I discovered that early on. Still, Justin went behind my back to show you this dump. A fatal mistake."

She opened a drawer and took out a cell phone, staring at the too-bright screen. "I'm going to make the rounds and then I'm leaving."

Gavin gave Brianne a warning glance. "You're right, Liza, we are cops and we've got this building surrounded. You walk out of here, and you'll be shot on the spot."

Liza went pale but motioned to her brother. Bill held the gun closer. Close enough for Brianne to know this man was the Tick. "Bill?"

She stood, too, but Liza pushed her back down.

"If you move, I'll start the fireworks right now."

"Fireworks?" Brianne looked around. "What are you talking about?"

"In fifteen minutes, something tragic will happen here," Liza replied, calm again. "An unfortunate accident. Another gas leak or maybe a faulty wire in the mechanical room. Holding up her phone, she said. "I just call it in. Boom. Boom."

Rushing around them, she opened the door and screamed, "Run, Bill! Get out!"

Bill, who had never uttered a word, did as his bossy sister asked. He handed her the gun and took off running.

Liza held the gun as she backed out the door. "So nice *not* doing business with you, Officers."

Then she slammed the door shut and Brianne heard the clicking of a lock.

"Gavin?"

"I know." He did a mic check. "Freddie, did you get all of that? She's onto us."

"Got it. We're moving in."

Gavin unleashed the dogs and told them to Find. "By the way, we're locked in and there's a bomb about to go off in this building." He gave their location.

Gavin and Brianne went into action. The dogs alerted on the armoire in the corner of the hot, tiny office. Tommy touched his paw to the door and whined. Stella sniffed the door handle and turned to stare at Brianne.

Gavin shot Brianne a look that told her everything she needed to know. He loved her. She saw it there in his dark eyes.

This man loved her. Too much.

He'd die for her.

"Gavin?"

"Bree, I'm going to open the door. We have to know what we're dealing with here."

She nodded, held back tears.

"Get behind the desk," he said. "Keep the dogs with you."

"Gavin, wait."

Then they heard something. A soft moan coming from the cabinet where the dogs had alerted.

"Get back, Bree."

Gavin pulled out his hidden weapon and gently opened the door to the closet-like cabinet.

Then he stood back.

Brianne looked up over the desk and gasped.

Justin Sanelli was tied up in the cabinet.

And he had a bomb strapped to his stomach.

Gavin turned to Brianne, a million scenarios going through his head. "We have to get this thing off of him."

Justin moaned, his eyes wide with fear. Gavin didn't try yet to remove the tape covering his mouth.

"Listen, Justin. Listen to me, okay?" Gavin leaned close, studying the three bars of C4 strapped and wired across Justin's midsection. "We're with the NYPD, understand? We're going to get you out of here, do you hear me?"

Justin moaned again and gave a slight nod, but the fear in his eyes didn't go away. He tried to say something.

Sirens sounded all around. Loud shouts echoed through the building.

"Our backup is here." Gavin turned to Brianne. "I'm going to get this tape off."

She nodded, her weapon drawn, the dogs behind her. "I'll work on the door."

Gavin turned back to Justin. "Don't move," he said. "And don't scream."

Justin moaned again. Gavin counted to three and yanked off the tape, praying all the way.

Justin didn't scream, but he started talking. "She's a madwoman. She thinks I'm in cahoots with you. She's a bomb-maker. How can I work for a woman and not know that she's the one who's been sabotaging half the buildings we buy? And how could I not see that you two are cops?"

"Calm down," Gavin said. "It's okay. We're gonna get you out of here but I need your help. We've only got about ten minutes."

"Do something!" Justin said, sweat covering his ruddy face. "She plans to blow us up with her phone."

"Is her brother involved?"

"He delivers the bombs, sets them up. But he's tired of her ordering him around. He messed up on the Fourth of July. Went to the wrong building and panicked."

"So he deliberately moved through the crowd at the fireworks," Gavin said to keep Justin talking. He could see the twisted wires on the bomb, the same loops and swirls as the others. They'd been after the wrong man.

The Tick was a woman.

"I don't know, but I heard them talking. He rarely talks to anyone but her. She's always bossed him around. But I know he did something she wasn't happy about."

"Just hang on, Justin. We'll be out of here soon."

Brianne touched Gavin's arm. "The door is solid and locked tight. Maybe the window."

Justin stared up at Gavin, sweat shimmering on his skin. "She'll go out the basement door to the street. You won't leave me?"

"I won't," Gavin said. Then he stood up and went to the window. After trying to pry it loose, he used the butt of his gun to knock out the old panes. Fresh air filled the room.

"Bree, send the dogs out and go with them."

"No. I won't do it."

Gavin saw the tears in her eyes and he also saw the bravery. "You need to get out of here. We don't have much time."

"No." She backed away, shaking her head. "Gavin, no."

He hurried to her, guiding her. "Get out, Brianne. I mean it."

She gave him a hurt look and then glanced at Justin. "I'm going to find Liza. I'll make sure she's put away for a long time, Justin."

Then before Gavin could warn her to be careful, she grabbed a chair and climbed up into the open window. She looked back once, her eyes holding his while she commanded the dogs to Go.

Gavin watched as she dropped down onto the ground into an alleyway, his heart breaking when she glanced back up at him. He might not see her again.

Turning back to Justin, he stared at the frightened man.

"Are you two the real deal?" Justin asked in a quiet voice.

Gavin nodded, cleared his throat. "Yeah, we are. We're the real deal."

TWENTY-TWO

Brianne wanted to take off her mic and throw it on the ground. She couldn't bear to hear the bomb exploding in her ear. But she had to report in and she needed backup, so she listened and prayed they'd get to Gavin in time.

She did, however, want to find Liza Collins. That need burned through Brianne and cut through the pain she'd seen in Gavin's eyes when he'd demanded she leave.

The woman's perfume had lingered in the air of that stifling little room, so she ordered the dogs to Search. Liza's scent—the scent they'd zoomed in on—was that of a bomber.

Tommy had tried to warn them at the open house. They'd misread his signals. And Stella had picked up the bomb's scent on William Caston—Bill—when he'd walked into the crowd to dispose of a bomb he'd taken to the wrong place—a bomb both his sister and he had handled.

She'd seen the whirls and twists of this bomb's wiring. Liza was an evil woman who had two major talents—selling real estate and making bombs. But her ego had given her away in the form of dainty bomb wiring.

Why hadn't they picked up on her sooner?

Because she'd used her own brother as a decoy and as her runner. She'd sent him through the open house to lure them away, already paranoid that they planned to take over her territory. What a horrible life Bill must have had, always lurking about doing her dirty deeds. Creepy and evil.

Brianne followed the dogs until she reached the back of

the old building. Another alleyway, but near the High Line.
She could hear people laughing not far away. But she also
heard sirens and, from the chatter coming through her ear-
bud, knew the bomb squad was in place. She heard Gavin
reassuring Justin. Checking her watch, she prayed they'd
make it in time. She couldn't think about what would happen if they didn't.

She radioed her location and followed the two K-9s, surprised when they reached Gansevoort and Tommy wanted
to go onto the High Line. Had Liza taken the popular green
space that used to be a train track?

A lot of places to hide there.

The dogs were rarely wrong, so Brianne ordered them
to keep going. They made it up the entryway and moved
through the crowds, the afternoon heat beaming down
on them.

Tears moved in a quiet stream down her face, but Brianne kept reporting her moves. They passed The Stan-
dard, High Line Hotel. She searched in all directions. How
would she ever find Liza in this crowd? Brianne looked to
the right, her heart doing that little flip when she thought
she saw Liza up ahead. They kept moving. The High Line
was a little over a mile long but she felt winded and fever-
ish in the heat, pushing past strolling people. She prayed
the dogs would hold out.

When they came near Chelsea Market, Tommy lifted
his snout and picked up the pace. The High Line cut underneath buildings here. Tommy alerted, and Stella soon
followed.

But where had Liza gone?

They moved to the Observation Deck after crossing
Tenth Avenue and Brianne stared down into the street
below. And she saw Liza strolling along, her phone in
her hand.

Five minutes. Liza had told them she'd hit the button in fifteen minutes and ten of those were gone. Liza would denotate the bomb if she couldn't get to her.

Five minutes to save Gavin and Justin.

"Gavin?" she said into her mic. "Officer Sutherland?"

"Bree?"

"I see her. Tenth Avenue Square. I'm going after her."

"Bree? Wait! Wait! I'm coming, I'm coming!"

"Are you out?"

"I'm still with Justin. The bomb squad is here. We've got eyes on you and the bomb squad is working to defuse the bomb. I promised Justin—"

"That you won't leave him."

"I promised, Bree. But I should be with you."

"I know, I can do this."

She hurried to the exit at 12th and 34th and then back-tracked. She came up on Liza sitting on a bench, watching her phone.

"It's over, Liza," Brianne said, easing closer with her weapon drawn.

The woman looked up without surprise. "No, you're wrong about that, *Reinhart*. I can't let you live. You're cops—Bill followed you two to a vacant building site, but he ran away when he heard a dog barking. Undercover cops—that's an uneven playing field, don't you think?" Holding the phone up, she said, "It won't be over until I finish it."

Liza gave Brianne a smug smile and put her finger to the phone.

Brianne moved in. "Drop the phone, Liza. Drop it or I'll shoot you."

Liza shook her head. "I don't really care about that right now. I just want to watch your face when the bomb explodes."

"Don't," Brianne said, holding her breath, expecting an explosion somewhere behind them. She prepared to make the shot.

Liza went to hit the button at about the same time Brianne shot her in the upper arm She wouldn't give the woman the satisfaction of a forced death-by-cop.

Liza screamed, blood seeping down her arm and onto her white pants.

Brianne waited, her heart pounding, tears blurring her eyes. The bomb didn't go off.

For a brief instant after the shot, birds scattered and people screamed and hurried away. but soon the city kept moving. Horns honked, dogs barked, sirens screamed and the sky was a brilliant blue.

Liza let go of the phone and grabbed at her bleeding arm, her gaze hitting on Brianne. "What have you done?"

"She's done her job" came a winded, masculine voice behind them. "She's bringing in the Tick. Finally."

Brianne didn't dare turn, but she gulped in a breath that she'd been holding for the last fifteen minutes. Gavin rushed forward and commanded Tommy to Guard.

His partner obeyed, growling at the stunned woman sitting on the bench.

"Where is my stupid brother?" Liza asked.

"Sitting in a NYPD squad car singing like a bird," Gavin explained as he hauled her up and cuffed her. "Take a good long look at this view, Liza. It'll be the last time you see it."

After that, everything went by like a movie in Brianne's mind. Gavin guided her to an ambulance to get her checked out. Stella stayed by her side, guarding her. Freddie rushed by, taking over for Gavin. Luke and Carter showed up, helping to get a screaming Liza to a waiting ambulance with a guard to escort her to the hospital. FBI agents swarmed the scene.

Brianne sat and heard people rushing by, talking. "Just heard about a bomb scare right here in Chelsea."

"They stopped it with seconds to spare."

"God bless those K-9 officers and the bomb squad."

"God bless New York City."

Brianne closed her eyes and held tight to Stella. *Thank You, Lord.*

She felt a warm hand on her cheek. "Gavin?"

"It's over, Bree," he said, taking her into his arms and holding her close. "It's over."

Two days later, Gavin sat in the training yard with Carter Jameson watching Carter's little six-year-old girl, Ellie, play with a hyper puppy.

"Daddy, we need to take this one home, too," the cute dark-haired child said.

"Sweetie, we already have two puppies, remember? We're running out of room."

Gavin felt for Carter. His wife had died during child-birth and the man still had the shadow of grief about him. And now his brother, too. All the more reason for Gavin to grab on to love and hold tight. Which he planned to do soon.

"What a week," Carter said, passing Gavin the dough-nuts someone had brought out to the picnic table earlier. "I wish I could keep Ellie this innocent and free forever."

"Yep," Gavin said, anxious to go and see Brianne. The chief had made them both take a day but Gavin had come by headquarters to sign reports and tie up loose ends be-fore he headed to her place.

"Hey, Gavin," Carter said, "we're all sorry about even thinking you could be involved in Jordy's death. Chalk it up to grief and shock, man." He extended his hand, hope in his eyes.

Gavin shook his friend's hand. "I get it and I'm sorry for not handling my ambition a little better. Jordan and I had our differences, but he was a good man. I won't stop searching for his killer."

Carter nodded. "Thanks for that. And now that we know there were two people on that roof the day you found Scrawny and you and Brianne almost got hit by that beam, we know someone out there wants to get the jump on us finding his killer."

"Also look into the shooting at Griffin's," Gavin said. "Liza Collins claims after Justin told her about us, she had her brother start following us. But she realized we were police officers the day her brother tracked us to that building. He told us another man was there with the dog. So we think the person who killed Jordan was behind the shooting at Griffin's. He started going after whomever he could find to keep us all guessing. However, the bombing there was set up deliberately—to threaten Brianne and me. Liza pulled out all the stops."

Carter nodded. "You and Brianne did a good job."

"Yeah, we make a good team," Gavin replied.

"In work or in life?" Carter questioned with a soft smile.

"We have a thing," Gavin admitted. Then he took a breath. "And if I have it my way, we'll be together for the rest of our lives."

"That's great," Carter said. "How are you gonna handle working together?"

"I've mulled that over," Gavin said. "I thought about asking for a transfer, so I talked to Noah and spilled my guts."

"And what did my brother say?"

"He told me I wasn't going anywhere and that both Bree

and I and our partners would be honored soon for stopping that bomber. We just can't work the same cases anymore."

"So a kiss every morning and off you go in different directions."

Seeing the pain in his friend's eyes, Gavin nodded. "I guess you were used to doing that, huh? Kissing your wife every morning."

"Yeah," Carter said. Then he looked at his little girl. "Now Ellie and I share that kiss." Turning back to Gavin, he added, "Grab tight, Gavin. Don't let go, okay?"

"I won't," Gavin said. "But first, I have to see how Brianne feels about this idea."

Carter laughed and stood up. "Well, what are you waiting for? Get going."

"Bree, you have a visitor."

Hearing her mother's words, Brianne turned from watching Stella chase yet another ball out in the backyard and saw Gavin walking toward her.

Her heart ran toward him before her feet could move. "Hi," she said, watching as Stella took off toward her friend Tommy and danced around him with delight.

"Hi," he responded when he met up with her near the swing underneath the old oak. "Got a minute?"

"I might," she said, motioning to the swing. "Come into my office and we'll check my schedule."

He sat down with her and smiled at their partners. "Those two knew right away, didn't they?"

"About the bomber? Yes."

"And about us, silly."

Her heart beat too fast. "Is there an 'us'?"

"I sure hope so," Gavin replied. "Justin Sanelli wants an invitation to our wedding and he's offered to give us a discount on a house, if we decide to buy a new one."

Letting that soak in, she asked, "Is he okay?"

"He will be. He'll testify against Liza Collins and her brother, William Caston—and he's been cleared of any wrongdoing. He thought his boss just had a talent for bringing in deals. He was clueless as to how she did it."

"Really?"

"Really, he's clean. He just bragged a bit too much and one of the people he bragged to was me, thankfully."

"Okay then." She looked Gavin in the eyes. "Now back to that other part…"

"You mean—how long will the wig-wearing bomb-toting twins stay behind bars?"

"No, I mean that part about a wedding and a house and…whatever comes after that."

Gavin turned and pulled her close, the old swing creaking.

"Do you want all of that, Bree? With me?"

"Is that your way of asking me to marry you?"

"We were good together as Linus and Alice, but don't expect designer purses or a penthouse in Manhattan, okay? But I do have a solid house and I will get you a ring, I promise."

"I'll take the ring and I can't wait to see the house. But the only thing I expect, Sutherland, is to spend the rest of my life coming home to you and those two amazing K-9s. Can you make that happen?"

"I've already worked out the plan," he said, telling her about his talk with Noah. "We're all clear."

"So…we're getting married?"

"We're getting married," he said, bringing her close. "I love you. I almost lost you."

"You almost lost yourself," she replied. "But I love you because you chose to stay with a frightened man strapped to a bomb when you knew you could die. That is a true hero, Gavin."

"And I love you because you did what I asked you to do—leave—and then went after an evil woman, knowing that you and I might not ever be together. That is a true heroine, Brianne."

She stared crying. "No aprons, okay?"

"No aprons. I'll cook for you, how about that?"

"I love you so much."

He kissed her and held her close. When they heard a loud squeal from inside the house, they pulled apart and started laughing.

"My mother," Bree said with a grin. "I sure am glad she didn't smack you too hard with that frying pan."

"So am I," he said. Then he stood and lifted her up and kissed her again. "Let's go inside. Your mom's making meatballs."

Together, they walked toward the house, their K-9 partners trotting behind them. Brianne glanced back and saw Stella giving Tommy a big doggie smile.

"I feel the same way, Stella Girl," she said, smiling over at Gavin. Looking up at the blue sky, she'd never felt more happy. Gavin had found peace at last and…a family who loved him.

* * * * *

If you enjoyed Deep Undercover, *look for Carter's story,*
Seeking the Truth, *coming up next and the rest of the*
True Blue K-9 Unit series from Love Inspired Suspense.
TRUE BLUE K-9 UNIT:
These police officers fight for justice with the help of
their brave canine partners

Dear Reader,

This was a challenging story, but I loved these characters and so enjoyed working with the other amazing authors in this series. New York City is an amazing place with one of the most dedicated police forces in the world. I hope I did them justice with this story.

Brianne was a go-getter while Gavin used caution. I believe our environments shape our personalities, so I tried to show that with these two very strong but different personalities. Please note that while I talked to several experts and did a lot of research on both New York and law enforcement, any mistakes are solely my own. God Bless the NYPD!

Please visit me at my website www.lenoraworth.com or chat with me on Facebook.

Until next time, may the angels watch over you. Always.

Lenora Worth